#5 Blubberina

Look for these and other books
in the Bad News Ballet series:

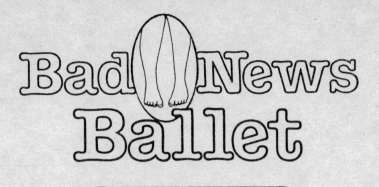

Bad News Ballet

#5 Blubberina

Jahnna N. Malcolm

AN
APPLE
PAPERBACK

SCHOLASTIC INC.
New York Toronto London Auckland Sydney

ISBN 0-590-42888-8

Copyright © 1989 by Jahnna Beecham and Malcolm Hillgartner. All rights reserved. Published by Scholastic Inc. APPLE PAPERBACKS is a registered trademark of Scholastic Inc.

12 11 10 9 8 7 6 5 4 3 2 1   9/8 0 1 2 3 4/9

Printed in the U.S.A.   11

First Scholastic printing, October 1989

Chapter One

"I have a big surprise for you all!" Annie Springer announced at the end of her Saturday ballet class.

A murmur of excitement rippled around the studio of the Deerfield Academy of Dance. Fourteen girls, each clad in a black leotard and pink tights, sat cross-legged on the hardwood floor and listened intently to their teacher.

The pretty dark-haired dancer folded her hands in front of her and smiled at the group of mostly fifth- and sixth-graders. "Next week Mr. Anton will visit our class."

The girls inhaled sharply. Mr. Anton was the stern director of the academy. He didn't visit their class very often but when he did, it was important.

"During that visit," their teacher continued, "he will decide which girls in our class will get their toe shoes."

"Toe shoes!" The room erupted into squeals of delight. Most of the girls had spent several years waiting for the moment, when at last they would be allowed to dance *en pointe.*

But not all of the girls in that Saturday class shared the same enthusiasm. Toward the back of the room, five young dancers sat huddled together in a tight little group.

One of them, a wiry girl with a thick mane of curly black hair, raised her hand. "Do we *have* to wear toe shoes?" Rocky Garcia asked. "I mean, what if we don't want to?" Rocky didn't like being pushed into anything.

Annie Springer's eyes widened in surprise. "Well, uh . . . no one will *force* you to wear them, but if you want to stay in this class, I think it would be a good idea."

Rocky turned back to her friends who were staring at her in shock and shrugged. "I just thought I'd ask."

Kathryn McGee leaned over and whispered, "If you ask me, it looks kind of painful. Jumping up and down on the tips of your toes? Ouch!"

"I'm with McGee," the plump red-haired girl sitting beside her muttered. "Squeezing our bodies into

2

these leotards once a week is torture enough. Do you want your feet to suffer, too?"

"I think it sounds truly romantic," Zan Reed murmured in her soft voice. The slim black girl hugged her knees to her chest. "Just imagine, twirling across the room on your toes!"

Gwen shoved her wire-rim glasses up on her nose and grimaced. "I'd probably get dizzy and throw up."

"Oh, you would not!" Mary Bubnik reached across the circle and swatted at Gwen. Then the curly headed blonde raised her hand and asked, "Will toe shoes make us real ballerinas, like you?"

Annie Springer was not only their teacher but a principal ballerina with the Deerfield Academy of Dance. She smiled and said, "Not quite, Mary. But it'll be a good start."

"My mother will be so excited," Mary gushed to her friends. "I think she's convinced I'm a permanent klutz."

Gwen raised an eyebrow but didn't say a word. Mary Bubnik may be one of her best friends but there was no denying she *was* a klutz. If Mary wasn't tripping over her own feet, she was stepping on someone else's. The very thought of Mary Bubnik tottering around on toe shoes seemed disastrous.

"Miss Springer?" A very pretty girl sitting by the piano raised her hand. She smoothed a strand of her brown hair into the tight bun on her head.

"Yes, Courtney?"

"Some of us already have our toe shoes," Courtney Clay gestured toward the two girls sitting beside her. With their perfect buns and matching dancewear, all three looked like clones of each other.

"Yes, I'm well aware of that," Annie said, smiling pleasantly.

"Well, what will *we* do?" Page Tuttle, the pale blonde next to Courtney, asked. "Since we're so much better — I mean, more advanced than the others."

"Make me gag." Gwen shoved a finger down her throat.

"Well, Page, as an advanced student," Annie Springer explained patiently, "I'm sure you're aware that you will do the same warm-up exercises as the rest of the class. But some advanced steps like the *channé* turns and *pirouettes* — you, Courtney, and Alice will be able to try *en pointe*."

Courtney turned to her friends and whispered loudly, "I've already done those steps on my own."

"So have I," Page Tuttle replied quickly.

"Me, too," Alice added in her nasal voice.

"Is it hard getting way up to the end of your toes?" one of the other girls in the class asked.

"There's nothing to it," Courtney cried, springing to her feet. "See?" She raised up *en pointe* and then *bourréed* in little tiny steps across the floor. Page and Alice hurried to join her and the three girls demonstrated the steps in a line.

4

While most of the class oohed and ahhed, the gang huddled together in a tight group.

"Look at those Bunheads," Rocky grumbled. "They think they're so cool."

"What a bunch of show-offs." Gwen glared at the trio in irritation. "They only have their toe shoes because they've been taking classes longer than us."

"And because they actually *like* ballet," Rocky pointed out.

"That's right," McGee said, flipping one of her braids over her shoulder. "The only reason we decided to take classes here at the academy was so we would be sure and see each other once a week."

"And stay the best of friends," Zan concluded.

The gang had first met in December, when their mothers had forced them to try out for the Deerfield Academy of Dance's production of *The Nutcracker*. Even though the girls went to different schools around the city they had formed a bond of friendship that they swore would never break.

McGee pointed to Courtney and Page, who were still parading around in front of the class. "I wouldn't mind getting toe shoes," she said, "just to show the Bunheads that we're as good as they are."

"It might be kind of cool," Rocky agreed. "You'd be taller than everyone and able to kick a lot higher." She leaped into the air and let loose a swift karate kick with her right leg. "It could also be a plus in defending yourself."

"Ballerinas are truly the most beautiful dancers of all," Zan sighed dreamily. She closed her eyes and imagined herself dancing lightly on the tips of her toes across a stage. Just as quickly she saw herself tripping and embarrassing herself in front of thousands of people, and her eyes popped open wide.

"I don't know," Gwen shook her head. "I just don't think it's possible for those little satin shoes to hold up your entire body weight."

"It isn't," Courtney Clay remarked loudly. "Especially when you look like Miss Piggy." She turned and whispered snidely to Page and Alice, "Her toes would probably break off from the strain."

Rocky overheard the remark and snapped, "Yo, Courtney! One more crack like that, and you'll be eating a knuckle sandwich."

Courtney stopped laughing and glared at Rocky. "You can't scare me. You try something like that, and I'll tell."

Rocky folded her arms across her chest and her dark eyes flashed. "Who are you gonna tell, your mother?"

Cornelia Clay was on the board of directors for the Deerfield Academy of Dance. She was wealthy and had a lot of influence in the academy, which Courtney never let anybody forget.

Courtney looked down her nose at Rocky. "Maybe."

"I'm scared." Rocky quivered her hands in front of Courtney's face. "Look, I'm shaking."

McGee grabbed Rocky by the sleeve and pulled her away. "C'mon, Rocky, they're not worth the trouble."

"I just don't like to hear them say crummy things about my friends," Rocky grumbled.

McGee patted her friend on the back. "Me, neither."

"All right, class dismissed." Miss Springer clapped her hands together sharply. "We'll see all of you next week. And good luck!"

The room exploded with sound as all of the dancers crowded through the studio door. Everyone was chattering about the big news. The gang all grabbed their dance bags and hurried out into the lobby, where their friend Miss Delacorte worked at the reception desk.

"We're getting our toe shoes!" Mary Bubnik announced.

"This is such wonderful news!" the elderly lady trilled in her Russian accent. "We will make *real* ballerinas of you yet."

"Plié. Relevée," the black bird on her shoulder squawked. "Hooray!"

"See?" Miss Delacorte laughed. "Miss Myna is proud of you, too."

"Just imagine," Mary Bubnik gushed. "Me — *en*

pointe!" She attempted a turn in the middle of the room and crashed into the pedestal by the door.

"Look out!" McGee shouted. The vase of flowers on top of the pedestal wobbled dangerously and McGee caught it just in the nick of time.

"What a klutz," Courtney chortled from the curtain of the dressing room.

Rocky spun around angrily, ready to start their fight all over again when Mary giggled, "You're right. I am a klutz!"

"By the way, I wouldn't get too excited about toe shoes," Courtney called, leaning casually against the door sill. "Mr. Anton has to check you over first to see if you qualify." She patted her hair smugly. "Frankly, I don't think you will."

"What happens if we don't?" Mary Bubnik asked.

Courtney shrugged. "You'll probably be transferred to a lower class."

"Awwk!" Miss Myna squawked. "Button your lip!"

Courtney wrinkled her nose. "That bird is disgusting. I don't know why Mr. Anton lets you bring it here."

Miss Delacorte gently stroked the bird's ruffled feathers. "Most of the students like her."

"Well, I don't!" She looped her dance bag over her shoulder and marched out of the studio.

"And I don't like Courtney," Rocky grumbled. "So we're even."

Zan turned to the receptionist and asked, "Is it true what Courtney said? That we might not get our toe shoes?"

"Well . . . yes." Miss Delacorte rubbed her chin thoughtfully. "Sometimes your ankles aren't strong enough. Sometimes your weight may not be right."

Gwen, who was in the middle of biting into a chocolate bar, gulped.

"And sometimes Mr. Anton may decide you need another year of training," Miss Delacorte finished.

A dark cloud of gloom settled over the gang. Finally McGee said what they were all thinking. "It would really be embarrassing if we didn't get our toe shoes."

Rocky nodded glumly. "The Bunheads would never let us live it down."

"Now you are all so very blue." Miss Delacorte shut the drawer of her desk with a bang and stood up. "I think what you need is a nice cup of tea and some treats."

"What kind of treats?" Gwen asked, licking the chocolate off her fingers.

"Marzipan cookies."

Gwen's eyes lit up. "I feel better already!"

"Then it's settled. You girls hurry and change into your street clothes, and then we will go to my house, yes?"

"Be my guest!" Miss Myna croaked. Miss Dela-

9

corte picked up a little gilded cage from beside the file cabinet and set it on top of her desk. She opened the wire door and the myna bird fluttered down from her shoulder and hopped inside. Then Miss Myna screeched, "Follow me! Awwk!"

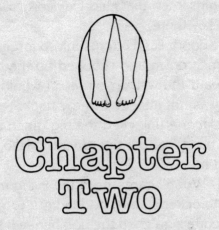

Chapter Two

Miss Delacorte lived in an old brick building just behind Hillberry Hall. Her apartment was on the third floor.

"When are they going to put an elevator in this building?" Gwen huffed as she followed the others up the winding marble stairs.

"Never, I hope," Miss Delacorte replied, searching in her large tapestry bag for her house key. "The exercise is good for you."

She handed the bird cage to McGee and then patted her pockets systematically. The girls watched as Miss Delacorte riffled through her purse a second time. It was a ritual the old woman went through every time they visited her.

Zan smiled patiently at their absent-minded friend. "Did you check under the doormat?" she asked tactfully. The girls knew that Miss Delacorte always kept her spare key there.

"Oh, my goodness, I am get-ink so forgetful!" The old lady knelt down and scooped up the brass key from beneath the welcome mat. "I would lose my brain if it was not attached to my neck."

Miss Delacorte unlocked the big green door and stuck her head into the apartment. "Hello, my darlinks, I am home!"

A joyful "Woof!" came from the living room and an ancient cocker spaniel padded out to greet her. Miss Delacorte scratched the dog beneath her white muzzle and cooed, "My lee-tle Sasha! Were you a good girl today?"

The beaded curtain in the door to the living room rustled as a fat orange cat with no tail came bounding out. A black-and-white cat was right behind him.

"Misha!" Miss Delacorte scolded gently. "You should not be chasing Mr. Stubbs in the house." The cats ignored her and rubbed around her ankles, mewing softly.

Zan was the first of the girls to step inside the apartment. She paused in the doorway and took a deep breath. "It always smells delicious here. Like cinnamon and roses, all mixed together in a wonderful bouquet."

"Go into the living room and make yourselves at

home," Miss Delacorte instructed. "I will put on the kettle for our tea, and then I want to show you all something very special."

"I'll help you with those cookies," Gwen volunteered, hurrying after Miss Delacorte into the kitchen. The rest of the girls hung their jackets on the ornate wooden coatrack in the foyer, then made their way into the living room. A Persian rug lay on the floor in front of the fireplace. The mantle was lined with little framed photographs, yellowing with age.

"I love it here," Zan said as she sank into the velvet-covered couch by the window. Misha the black-and-white cat sprang into her lap and curled up in a purring ball of fur. "It's truly like stepping into another time period."

"No kidding," Rocky said as she tweaked one of the gold tassels hanging from the thick red brocade curtains across the windows. "Everything's about a hundred years old."

"Sort of like Miss Delacorte," Gwen cracked as she set a tray of almond cookies on the coffee table. She glanced hurriedly over her shoulder as Miss Delacorte crossed into the back of the apartment. Then she stuffed two cookies into her mouth.

McGee put a record on the old Victrola in the corner and wound the hand crank. Soon the scratchy sounds of an old recording of *Swan Lake* wafted from the fluted horn of the record player.

Suddenly a loud crash sounded from the bedroom and the girls looked up in alarm.

"My goodness, but that hurt!" Miss Delacorte shrieked.

Rocky raced into the bedroom and found Miss Delacorte sitting on the floor in front of her closet. The floor around her was littered with shoeboxes, old valises, and scraps of tissue paper. She had one hand pressed to her forehead.

"Are you OK?" Rocky cried.

"I opened the closet and all of these things fell right on my head," Miss Delacorte gasped.

"Do you want me to pick this up?" Rocky asked, kneeling down beside her.

"No, no, I'll get it later." Miss Delacorte rested her chin on her palm and stared at the mess. "It's about time I did some spring cleaning, don't you think?"

"Sounds like a good idea," Rocky agreed.

Miss Delacorte crawled on her hands and knees into the closet. "I'm looking for one little box." She tossed some old newspapers over her shoulders and then cried out, "Aha! Here it is!"

She passed a black satin case with elaborate embroidery on it over her shoulder to Rocky, who stared at it uncomprehendingly. It looked like a jewelry box of some sort, or a purse.

Rocky held the case up and shook it. "What's in here, anyway?"

Grabbing the doorknob of the closet, Miss Delacorte nimbly pulled herself to her feet. "I will show you." She picked her way through the debris on the floor and together they went back into the living room.

"And now, girls, come see!" Taking the box out of Rocky's hands, the old lady set it down in the middle of the little coffee table in front of the couch. "Here is one of my oldest treasures."

The girls gathered around on their knees. Miss Delacorte gently opened the case. The tissue paper inside had once been pink but had now faded to a dusty yellow. "Here they are," Miss Delacorte announced proudly, "my very first pair of toe shoes."

The gang gasped as she held up the tiniest pair of satin slippers that any of them had ever seen. The pink satin had lost much of its sheen and the worn toes were traced with lines of different-colored thread where they had been darned.

"Oh, I was so young," Miss Delacorte whispered softly. The girls looked up to see her eyes glistening. "And yet I remember the moment I got these like it was yesterday."

The kettle began to whistle and Miss Delacorte rose to her feet. "I'll go get the tea." She hurried out of the room dabbing at her eyes with a white handkerchief.

After she had gone, Gwen held up one of the tiny slippers in the light. "Wow. Talk about little. These look like shoes for a midget."

Mary Bubnik nodded. "It's hard to believe any-body's foot could ever be that small."

"And feel them," McGee said, squeezing the tip of the shoe. "There's nothing there at all."

"It's like dancing in a satin sock," Zan murmured.

Gwen winced. "Just thinking about it makes my toes hurt."

"Here we are!" Miss Delacorte floated back in carrying a large tray that held a large silver cannister covered with floral engravings. China teacups were clustered around its base. "I decided to use the sam-ovar. Russian tea should *only* be served in a Russian teapot."

Miss Delacorte set down the samovar and poured them each a cup of tea.

"Didn't these shoes hurt your feet?" Mary Bubnik asked.

"Oh, my, yes," the old woman laughed. "Many times I would go home with bleeding toes."

Gwen choked on her marzipan cookie. "Your toes bled? I don't like the sound of that at all."

Miss Delacorte patted Gwen on the shoulder. "Don't worry, my little friend. Shoes are made of much better material now. And even if your toes do bleed at first, they soon develop callouses and be-come strong."

Zan cradled the lovely delicate slippers in her hands. "I can't believe you've kept these all these years."

16

"They have been — how do you say? My good luck charms," the old lady replied. "I never go anywhere without them."

Zan set the slippers back into the box, her slim, brown fingers lingering on the ribbons. "I wish I had a lucky charm," she said softly. "I could truly use one."

McGee tilted her head. "Why?"

Zan took a deep breath and blurted out, "Monday night is the all-city spelling bee, and I'm representing Stewart Elementary in the finals."

"What!" McGee shrieked so loud she startled the animals. Miss Myna cawed and flapped around the room while the cats raced for cover under the furniture.

"Way to go, Zan!" Rocky shouted. "That's terrific!"

"You mean all of the schools around Deerfield are in this contest?" Mary Bubnik asked, blinking her big blue eyes.

Zan looked down at her teacup and nodded.

"That's a very big deal!" Gwen said. "Why didn't you tell us?"

"I was embarrassed." Zan's cheeks grew bright red. "Besides, I probably won't win."

"What do you mean?" Rocky asked. "You've studied, haven't you?"

"Of course I have," Zan replied. "That's all I've done for the past month." Then she shuddered. "But the thought of standing up in front of all of those strangers has got me petrified."

17

"Spell that," Gwen commanded.

Zan snapped to attention. "Petrified. P-E-T-R-I-F-I-E-D — petrified."

Everyone applauded and Zan smiled with pleasure. Rocky punched her on the shoulder, "You'll win, no problem."

"I wish I had your confidence," Zan murmured.

"Spell that," Mary Bubnik teased.

Once again Zan sat up straight and rattled off, "Confidence. C-O-N-F-I-D-E-N-C-E — confidence."

The gang stared at her blankly. Finally Gwen asked, "Uh . . . is that right?"

"How would I know?" McGee shrugged. "She's the spelling champ."

Rocky nodded at Zan proudly. "Sounded good to me."

Miss Delacorte, who had been quietly sipping her tea while the girls talked, set her cup down on its saucer with a clatter. "I am thinking I know what your problem is, Zan. And I have the *perfect* thing to help you."

The old woman hurried off toward the bedroom, her purple chiffon scarf trailing behind her like the tail of a kite. "If I could just remember where it was."

"Don't go into the closet," Rocky warned.

"Don't worry," Miss Delacorte called over her shoulder, "this treasure is too precious to keep in the closet."

Moments later the girls heard another loud crash,

18

followed by a sharp yelp. "My, my, that was a close one!"

Miss Delacorte limped back into the living room, clutching a small wooden box in her hands. "That old bed almost broke my foot." Miss Delacorte sat on the overstuffed couch and patted the seat next to her. "Come here, Zan, and I will show you something very wonderful."

Zan obeyed and looked at the wooden box expectantly.

"You said you needed luck?" Miss Delacorte tapped the lid of the old box with her finger. "This, my friend, is the luckiest thing I have."

"That old box?" Gwen mumbled as she took a big bite of her cookie.

"Ah-ah-ah!" Miss Delacorte lifted one bony finger. "As they say, never judge a book by its cover. Inside this box is the Amber Stone worn by Anastasia!"

"Who's that?" McGee asked.

"Who was Anastasia?" Miss Delacorte put her hands to her heart in dismay. "Only a princess of the royal house of Romanov. She was the daughter of Nicholas and Alexandra, the last emperor and empress of Russia. Unfortunately, Anastasia was the only child of that family to survive the Revolution."

"What happened to the others?" Gwen asked.

"They were shot by the Bolsheviks." Miss Delacorte shook her head sadly. "Such a tragedy."

"All of them?" Mary Bubnik asked, wide-eyed.

Miss Delacorte nodded. "Including Anastasia."

"I don't get it," Rocky said. "How did she live if she was shot?"

"It was the Amber Stone," Miss Delacorte explained, her eyes aglow. "It saved her life." As she spoke Miss Delacorte removed the lid of the wooden box.

The girls crowded in to get a peek. They had expected to see an elaborate piece of jewelry inlaid with diamonds, emeralds, and rubies. But all they saw was a large honey-colored pebble sitting on a faded green velvet cushion.

"But that just looks like an old rock," Mary Bubnik said in disappointment.

"Yeah," McGee agreed. "It's even got a chip in it."

"Ah, but that is what makes it so lucky." Miss Delacorte picked up the stone and traced the long gash on its surface with her fingernail. "Anastasia was wearing this around her neck when the Bolsheviks broke into her family's palace and murdered them. The bullet meant for Anastasia's heart hit this stone instead — and she lived!"

The girls looked back at the stone with new wonder. The curtain rustled from the breeze outside and a ray of sunlight played across the gem's smooth surface, making it glow with a special intensity.

"Look!" Mary Bubnik cried. "It looks like it's got its own light inside."

"As if it were alive with magic," Zan murmured in a hushed whisper.

The girls stared down at the gem in speechless awe. Finally McGee asked, "How long ago did this happen?"

"That was in 1918," Miss Delacorte replied. "And since then, this magical stone has brought good fortune to whoever possessed it. A friend of the royal family gave it to me when I was leaving Russia." She replaced the lid and carefully set the box in Zan's hands. "Now I give the Amber Stone of Anastasia to you, Zan." The old woman's voice quivered with emotion. "Protect it with your life, and believe in it with your heart. It will bring you good fortune, I am sure."

Zan cradled the box in her lap and her eyes filled with tears. "Thank you, Miss D."

Miss Delacorte patted her on the shoulder and then she rose to her feet. "I will go bring you more marzipan cookies."

The moment she was out of sight, Mary Bubnik gushed, "You're already lucky, Zan." When Zan looked at her perplexed, Mary explained, "To be chosen to be the Keeper of the Amber Stone of Anastasia. I am *so* jealous!"

"You don't really believe all that stuff, do you?" Rocky asked, leaning back against the brass grate of the fireplace. "I mean, it just looks like an old chipped rock to me."

McGee and Gwen exchanged looks. Then McGee shrugged and said, "I don't know . . ."

"I believe in it," Mary Bubnik declared. "I know it will make Zan win that spelling bee on Monday night." She smiled at the rest of the group. "And I'm going to be there to watch her do it."

"Hey, we should all go," McGee said, finishing the last of her tea. "Just to root for Zan."

Zan, who had been sitting quietly, staring at the box in her hands, suddenly stood up. "I have to go home now." Her voice had a distant, dreamy sound. "You see, I truly have to study."

Zan drifted to the front door as if in a trance. She slipped her dark red cape over her shoulders and then turned and called, "Farewell!"

Gwen made a face at the rest of the group and repeated, *"Farewell?"*

As if in answer, Zan stuck her head back around the corner of the door and spelled, "F-A-R-E-W-E-L-L — farewell." Then with a huge grin and a wave she was gone.

Chapter Three

On Monday night, the gang stood huddled in the lobby of the Masonic auditorium. The carpeted foyer was crowded with parents and kids shoving and pushing their way into the aisles of the theatre to get the best seats. McGee peered through the big glass doors into the darkness outside. "I wonder what's keeping Rocky?"

"I don't know," Gwen grumbled, "but she'd better get here soon. The spelling bee's about to start."

"Boy, oh, boy," Mary Bubnik drawled, "I've never seen so many kids in my life. They've come from all over the city."

Gwen dug into the pocket of her wool coat and pulled out a bright yellow bag. "Here, have an M&M.

They'll help us make it through this contest — I understand these things can go on forever."

McGee shook her head. "I bet it'll be over pretty fast."

Gwen paused with a handful of candy halfway to her mouth. "What makes you say that?"

McGee pointed to a cordoned-off area on the left side of the lobby. A number of boys and girls with name tags on their chests paced around nervously while a woman carrying a clipboard bustled among them, giving last minute instructions.

"You see that girl with the thick glasses and frizzy brown hair?" McGee said.

The others nodded.

"That's Cecile Gillespie. She's Zan's biggest competition."

"How do you know that?" Mary Bubnik asked.

"Because Cecile goes to my school, and she happens to be a major brain," McGee explained. "She's made straight A's since the day she entered kindergarten."

"Wow!" Mary Bubnik shook her head in awe. "That's amazing."

"Hmmph!" Gwen shoved her glasses up on her nose and crossed her arms. "Cecile hasn't got a chance."

"What are you talking about?" McGee challenged.

Gwen moved closer to the velvet railing. "See the short, scrawny guy in the blue blazer standing next to Cecile? That's Barry 'The Brain' Brownlee. He just happens to go to *my* school."

"So?" McGee said.

"Barry takes his math and science classes at the high school," Gwen replied. "People call him a genius."

"Wait a minute!" Mary Bubnik tugged at their sleeves. "Do you see the girl in the green coat and red knee socks?"

"Where?" Gwen and McGee squinted at the group.

Mary pointed in the opposite direction. "By the water fountain." They watched a small girl stand on tiptoe to get a drink of water.

"Is she smart?" McGee asked.

Mary Bubnik shrugged. "I have no idea. I've just seen her at recess. I don't even know her name."

Gwen stared at Mary in confusion. "What does that have to do with the spelling bee?"

"Nothing." Mary Bubnik smiled. "I just thought you'd like to know that some people from my school came to this thing, too."

"Geez Louise! Get serious!" McGee flipped one of her chestnut braids over her shoulder. "We were discussing the fact that Zan is about to get creamed in front of thousands of people."

"How can you say that?" Mary Bubnik said. "Zan is smart, too. She's just a fifth-grader and she's representing her whole elementary school. That means

25

she beat out everyone in the sixth grade."

"That's true," Gwen admitted. "But Barry Brownlee is a major brain."

"And so is Cecile," McGee added.

"You guys are forgetting one very important thing." Mary Bubnik looked both ways, then said in a low voice, "Zan's got the Amber Stone of Anastasia."

"I've been thinking about that stone." Gwen popped another handful of M&Ms in her mouth and chewed thoughtfully. "Miss Delacorte is awfully nice but sometimes I think she's missing a few screws. I mean, as far as I'm concerned, that stone is just a chipped rock."

"That stone saved Anastasia," Mary Bubnik announced firmly. "And it will make Zan win."

"I hope so, 'cause look over there." McGee gestured with her thumb to the far side of the cordoned area. Zan was leaning against the wall, intensely studying a gray pamphlet. Every few seconds she would close her eyes and her lips would move.

"Zan's still trying to cram for the contest," Gwen moaned, "and Barry the Brain and Cecile aren't even studying."

"Yoo-hoo, Zan!" Mary called across the crowded room.

Zan just kept staring into her book. Finally McGee put two fingers in her mouth and whistled. A shrill blast of sound split the air. For a moment everyone in the lobby froze, including McGee.

26

Gwen blinked out at all the people staring at them. "Way to go," she muttered. "We're here five minutes and you've already created a scene."

McGee stared at her fingers in astonishment. "I can't believe it. I've never been able to whistle that loudly before."

"Well, at least it got Zan's attention," Mary Bubnik said as the crowd started talking again. "She's looking in our direction." Mary hopped up and down, waving. "Zan, over here!"

Zan blinked her big brown eyes and a slow smile of recognition crossed her lips. Mary Bubnik raised her arms in a V for Victory and McGee gave her the thumbs-up. Then the lady with the clipboard started ushering the contestants through the side aisle door into the auditorium.

Mary Bubnik put one hand over her chest. "My heart is pounding in my chest. You'd think I was going up on that stage with her."

"Hey, where'd everybody go?" McGee spun in a circle. "The lobby's almost deserted."

"You girls better take your seats," an usher hissed at them. "The spelling bee is about to start."

"But we're waiting for a friend," Mary Bubnik protested. "She'll never find us if we go in now."

The usher pointed to the far end of the lobby. "Then wait in the lounge. And don't make any noise."

The lounge wasn't much, just a gray couch, a few stainless steel ashtrays, and three large potted palms. The girls hurried over to the tiny alcove and positioned themselves on the gray couch so they could watch the entrance.

"If Rocky doesn't get here soon," Gwen grumbled, "Zan may have been eliminated, and we'll never get to see her in action."

"Pssst! You guys!" a voice whispered.

"Did you hear something?" Mary Bubnik asked. Mystified, the girls looked around the lobby.

"Over here!" the voice repeated.

McGee stared intently at the potted plant nearest the window. "It sounds like it's coming from over there."

"Oh, yeah?" Gwen laughed. "There's nothing there but a ratty old palm tree."

"Well, look again," McGee said. "That ratty old tree is wearing red hi-tops."

Peeking out from the base of the tree were a familiar pair of bright red sneakers. Mary Bubnik tiptoed up to the tree and whispered, "Rocky, is that you?"

"Yeah," a hoarse voice replied. "But don't come any closer."

"Why?"

"I need to get to the bathroom," Rocky replied, "but I'm afraid someone from my school might see me."

"Nobody's in the lobby," Gwen said. "The spelling bee's already begun."

Rocky peeked out from behind the tree. She was wearing her sunglasses but the right lens was badly cracked and the frames were bent out of shape. She held a tissue over her face.

"What on earth happened to you?" Mary Bubnik gasped.

Rocky lowered the tissue, revealing a bloody nose. "Russell Stokes."

"Did he hit you?" McGee asked.

"I don't want to talk about it," Rocky snapped.

"We'd better get to the bathroom before that usher sees you and makes you leave." Gwen peered around the edge of the alcove. She spotted the sign for the ladies room a few feet away and gestured for the others to follow her.

Once inside, they ran straight through the lounge to the area where the sinks were. McGee pulled several paper towels out of the dispenser and ran them under cold water. "Here, hold these up to your nose."

Rocky, who had been acting cool, suddenly saw her reflection in the mirror and turned white. "I look awful!" As she spoke the lens of her sunglasses fell out and clattered to the tiled floor. "Oh, no, these are my brother's. He's going to kill me."

"Not when he finds out you were mugged," Mary Bubnik said. "I think we should call the police."

"I wasn't mugged," Rocky muttered. "I was in a fight."

Just then the door of the ladies room swung open

and the girls could hear voices in the outer lounge.

"I just don't think it's fair," a woman was saying angrily. "They gave poor Deirdre a word that *I* can't even spell."

"I don't know what I'm going to say to Thomas," another woman sniffed. "After all the studying he did — to be eliminated on the very first word. It just breaks your heart. He'll probably never get over it."

Gwen peeked her head around the door and saw two middle-aged women in the lounge fixing their hair. "Excuse me," she asked, "is the spelling bee over already?"

"No," a woman in a polka dot dress replied, "but it might as well be." She slammed her hair brush down on the counter of the little vanity table. "I just don't think it's fair."

"How many contestants are left?" Gwen asked.

"Five," the other woman replied. "At least that's how many were there when we left the auditorium." She turned to her friend and huffed, "I don't know how they expect fifth- and sixth-graders to know such big words. It's scandalous."

"Five?" McGee gasped. "I hope we're not too late."

"Zan'll never forgive us if we miss her," Mary Bubnik moaned.

"What are we waiting for?" Rocky tossed the paper towels into the trash can. "Let's go."

Chapter Four

"Wow," McGee whispered as the five girls stepped into the back of the darkened auditorium. "The place is packed. There isn't an empty seat anywhere."

"We can just stand in the back," Gwen suggested.

Suddenly Mary Bubnik started punching them on the shoulders.

"Ow! Stop it," Rocky hissed. "That's sore."

Mary wasn't listening and kept gesturing toward the stage. "I can't believe it! There are only three contestants left, and Zan is one of them."

McGee and the others looked up and gasped. On the wide stage a row of folding chairs sat empty except for three right in the middle, where a boy and two girls stared nervously out at the audience. Off

31

to the left two judges sat behind a heavy wooden table.

"Oh, no," McGee groaned. "It's Straight A's Gillespie."

"And Barry 'The Brain' Brownlee." Gwen shook her head in despair. "Zan's a dead duck."

A man in the last row turned in his seat and angrily shushed the girls. Mary lowered her voice to a whisper. "Remember, Zan has the Amber Stone of Anastasia."

"What stone?" Gwen hissed. "I don't see it."

"Me, neither," McGee said. "Zan must not be wearing it."

"There it is," Rocky said, spotting the wooden box. "She's got it under the chair!"

The spectators turned and hushed them again. Cecile Gillespie stood up and walked up to the microphone standing center stage. Cecile received her word — *epidermis.*

"What's that mean?" Mary Bubnik whispered.

Gwen shoved her glasses up on her nose. "It means your skin and —" She looked up at the stage as a loud buzzer sounded. "It looks like Cecile spelled it wrong."

"I don't believe it," McGee said, as Cecile bowed gracefully and left the stage.

"The word now goes to the next contestant," the judge announced. The boy beside Zan rose to his feet and strode confidently toward the microphone.

"Uh — oh," Gwen hissed. "Here comes Barry the Brain."

Barry hiked up his trousers and, without hesitation, spelled, "E-P-I-D-E-R-M-I-S — epidermis."

The girls could tell by the smile on his face that he'd gotten the word right. There was a round of applause as Barry returned to his seat.

Now it was Zan's turn.

"I can't watch," Mary whispered, burying her head in McGee's shoulder. "It's too nerve-wracking."

"Well, at least she looks great," McGee whispered.

Zan smoothed her green velvet skirt nervously while the judges announced her word. Zan's eyes shone as she confidently spelled out her word. The judges nodded and the gang cheered loudly as Zan returned to her seat.

"Now what happens?" Mary Bubnik asked.

"They keep going until one of them blows it," Gwen replied, biting her lip nervously.

Barry and Zan traded words for several more rounds and, as the words grew harder, the tension became unbearable.

"The Sacred Amber Stone," Mary Bubnik murmured, clutching her hands to her chest. "The Sacred Amber Stone."

Soon all four of them were repeating it softly each time Zan had to spell a new word. She stumbled once on *renaissance* and Mary Bubnik almost fainted from fear. But Zan caught herself and finished the word successfully.

Suddenly it was Barry's turn again. He was given the word fluorescent. "F-L..." He hesitated, then went on, "U-O-R-E-S..." There was another long pause and the entire audience held its breath. Barry nervously wiped his forehead. Finally he declared, "S-E-N-T — fluorescent."

The buzzer sounded and the judge leaned forward once again. "I'm so sorry, Mr. Brownlee, but that is incorrect. Please wait in your seat until Miss Reed has completed her turn."

"Does that mean Zan wins?" Mary Bubnik squeaked.

"If she spells the word correctly, she does." McGee crossed her fingers and her legs, then folded her arms over her chest.

"C'mon, Zan," Rocky whispered. "You can do it."

Zan swallowed hard, then rose slowly from her chair. She pulled herself up to her full height and faced the microphone. The footlights blinded her and she couldn't see any of the faces in the crowd. She forced herself to think only of the word, concentrating on each letter at a time.

"F-L-U-O-R-E-S..." Zan's voice trailed off into silence.

Her mind had gone blank right at the spot where Barry Brownlee had messed up. Zan knew the word didn't have two s's because that was Barry's mistake. But what came next? She couldn't remember.

The audience shifted uneasily in their seats. A wave of panic rose up in her throat and for a second Zan was afraid she might faint. Then the image of the Amber Stone came into her mind, and she heard Miss Delacorte's soft voice whispering, "Believe in it with your heart."

Zan took a deep breath and calmly recited the rest of the word. "C-E-N-T — fluorescent."

There was a short silence and for a moment Zan wasn't quite sure whether she had spelled it right or not. She stared hard at the judges, waiting for their reply.

A broad smile creased the face of the chairman as he declared, "Ladies and gentlemen, we have a new all-city spelling champion. From the fifth grade at Stewart Elementary school — Ms. Suzannah Reed."

The auditorium erupted with applause, and McGee and Rocky led the others in a rousing cheer for their friend.

Zan's mother and father hurried up onto the stage and stood proudly beside Zan as she was awarded her first-place medal. Then a photographer from the *Deerfield Times* took her picture, first with the judges, then with her parents, then by herself.

The girls waited anxiously for her on the gray couch in the lobby. Fifteen minutes later Zan burst out of the auditorium and ran toward them, clutching her medal and the brown box in her hand.

"You did it," McGee yelled. "You beat Straight A's Gillespie."

"And Barry 'The Brain' Brownlee," Gwen added.

"And the entire city of Deerfield," Rocky and Mary Bubnik finished.

"I — I don't know what happened," Zan said. "My mind was a blank and then —" She held the wooden box out in front of her. "I thought of the Amber Stone. And I spelled the word right. It was truly a miracle!"

All five of them stared down at the little box with a new sense of wonder. "Wow," Mary Bubnik murmured. "It really is magical."

Even Rocky and Gwen seemed convinced. After a moment McGee said, "Maybe we should take it with us to class next Saturday when Mr. Anton tests us for our toe shoes."

"Good idea," Gwen and Rocky said together. Then just as quickly Gwen added, "I mean, it can't hurt."

Mary raised her hand. "Can I borrow it until then? I have a big test in geography on Friday and that's my worst subject. I could really use the Amber Stone's special power."

"Well, I don't know." McGee looked at Zan hesitantly. "Miss Delacorte did give it to Zan."

"I trust Mary," Zan said, her eyes glowing. "And I feel that this week she should be the Keeper of the Stone."

"The Keeper of the Stone," Mary Bubnik repeated solemnly.

McGee clapped her hands together. "I think we should have a special salute, or a secret ceremony, to make it more official."

"I like the sound of that," Rocky said. "What kind of a salute?"

McGee tugged on her pigtail thoughtfully. "I don't know."

"It should be something that a Russian princess would do without hesitation." Zan curtsied gracefully, extending the box out to Mary Bubnik. "I present to you the Amber Stone of Anastasia." Then she repeated Miss Delacorte's words breathlessly. "Protect it with your life, and believe in it with your heart."

Mary Bubnik imitated the curtsy, then pressed the box to her chest ecstatically. "I will!"

"Oooh, you guys," Rocky exclaimed suddenly, "I remember seeing this old movie where the natives brought gifts to their own sacred stone."

"Why'd they do that?" Gwen demanded, shoving her glasses up on her nose.

"To keep the gods happy," Rocky explained. "And to make their crops grow."

"Good." Zan lowered her voice dramatically. "Next week, each one of us should bring something to sacrifice to the sacred stone."

"Yeah!" McGee murmured.

"Like what?" Mary Bubnik asked.

"A precious possession," Zan explained in a hushed whisper. "Something that means a lot to you."

All of them nodded and turned toward the box Mary held in her hands. They bowed their head and intoned, "For the Amber Stone of Anastasia."

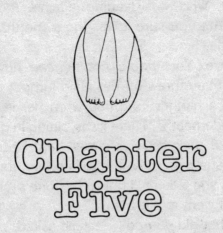

Chapter
Five

"It worked!" Mary Bubnik squealed as she entered the girls dressing room at the Deerfield Academy of Dance. The gang had agreed to meet early that Saturday and most of them had already arrived. Mary skipped over to the dressing table and very carefully placed the box on top of it.

"How did you do on your test?" McGee asked as she changed from her jeans into her black leotard and pink tights.

Mary Bubnik folded her hands in front of her and beamed at the group. "I got a C!"

"You got a C?" Gwen repeated as she stepped behind the standing mirror to change. "Is that good?"

"For me, it is," Mary replied. "I mean, I think it's a miracle that I even passed."

Rocky, who was leaning against the lockers, asked, "Are you sure it was the stone that got you that grade?"

"Positive. You would not *believe* how it happened." Mary threw off her plaid jumper and hung it up on a hanger. She had worn her leotard and tights underneath. "There I was, sitting in geography class, and that test was *super* hard." She stuffed some tissue paper into the toes of her floppy ballet shoes as she talked. "I got to this one problem and my mind went totally blank."

"So what did you do?" McGee asked.

"I put my hand on the box like this." Mary carefully placed her hand on the lid of the tiny wooden box. "And it was like someone had turned on a light in my brain. I suddenly remembered the capital of Indiana!"

"That's easy," Gwen said, poking her head out from behind the mirror. "It's Indianapolis."

Mary tossed her blonde curls petulantly. "Easy for you, maybe, but I'm not from around here." Mary and her mother had moved to Ohio just before school started. "Ask me what the capital of Oklahoma is. Now *that* I could tell you."

Just then Zan rushed into the dressing room. Her cheeks were flushed pink from running. "I'm truly sorry for being late," she breathed, "but I had a difficult time finding my special sacrifice."

"What did you come up with?" McGee asked.

Zan reached into the pocket of her red wool cape and pulled out a small parcel wrapped in brown paper. "This is the very first Tiffany Truenote mystery I ever read."

Tiffany Truenote was a teen detective that Zan idolized. She'd read every one of the books about her adventures many times over.

"Oh, that's a good one, Zan!" Mary Bubnik hugged her friend. "And really a sacrifice."

Zan set the book on the dressing table and bowed low to the box. "I give this book as an offering of gratitude to the Amber Stone of Anastasia."

Mary Bubnik removed a small framed photograph from her dance bag and, imitating Zan's voice and gestures, said, "I give this picture of my parents when they were happily married."

She lovingly placed it beside the box. The picture showed a man and a woman standing in front of a tidy white house. Between them, holding their hands and beaming at the camera, was a little blonde girl with curly hair. Her mother's divorce was the reason Mary Bubnik had moved to Deerfield, and it hadn't been easy adjusting to the change.

Mary bowed low and whispered, "Thank you for the C in geography, Anastasia. I will be eternally grateful."

Gwen looked at Rocky and stifled a giggle, then

opened her blue canvas dance bag. "Here is a jumbo size bag of peanut M&Ms *and* two packages of Twinkies." She removed a can of diet soda from her canvas bag. "And this is in case you get thirsty." Gwen bowed quickly from the waist and said, "Please help me — uh, *us* get our toe shoes today, OK?"

McGee looked at the candy skeptically. "That's what you call a sacrifice?"

"Yes." Gwen adjusted her glasses. "M&Ms and Twinkies just happen to be my favorite food."

"But you can get those anywhere."

"So?" Gwen crossed her arms and glared at McGee.

"So, I don't think they qualify as a precious personal possession."

Zan held up one hand and spoke in a dramatic whisper. "Each person must look to her own heart."

"And stomach," McGee muttered under her breath.

"If Gwen says it is a sacrifice," Zan continued, "then it is truly a sacrifice."

"Right," Gwen said emphatically. She gave McGee a dirty look. "I bet yours isn't any better."

McGee grabbed her backpack and pulled a dark round object out of the side pocket. She carefully placed it in front of the wooden box. "Oh, Amber Stone of Anastasia, please accept my lucky hockey puck, and help me get my toe shoes today." Then she added, "And please bring me luck at the little league tryouts Tuesday night. Thanks."

After she had finished her bow McGee turned and smiled smugly at Gwen. "Now *that's* a sacrifice."

Gwen rolled her eyes at the ceiling. "A beat-up old hockey puck. Big deal."

Finally it was Rocky's turn. She strolled forward and tossed a cassette tape onto the dressing table. "Yo, Anastasia! Here's my favorite tape — Death Star's greatest hits." As she walked back to the bench she muttered, "I'm not sure I believe in you but, just in case you are real, bring us our toe shoes today." Then she bowed quickly and flopped down on the bench.

"Well, look who's here," a voice sang out from the doorway of the dressing room. "It's the misfits."

The gang turned to see Courtney Clay smirking at them. Page Tuttle stood behind her, laughing haughtily. "And they're early," Page said. "I think they're trying to get brownie points with Mr. Anton."

"Well, it won't work." Courtney breezed past the gang and dropped her dance bag on the dressing table. "Mr. Anton only gives toe shoes to good dancers." She removed her pair of pink satin toe shoes as she spoke and placed them on the table.

"Yeah," Alice Wescott said in her high nasal voice, "only good dancers get to go *en pointe.*" She minced by the gang and joined Courtney and Page.

Courtney pointed at the dressing table. "Look at this junk. Doesn't anyone clean up around here?" With one hand she shoved the little wooden box and all of their gifts to one side.

"They must be for the lost and found." Page Tuttle picked up the hockey puck and examined it. "Miss Delacorte is in charge of that. She must have forgotten to collect them."

"That's typical," Courtney said as she tied the ribbons on her shoes.

McGee leaped forward and scooped the wooden box and their treasures up in her arms. "Um, those things are mine. I'll just move them over here."

She marched over to the far side of the room and carefully set the objects down on a bench. The rest of the gang hurried after her.

"Do you think it's true what Courtney says?" Mary Bubnik whispered, a worried frown on her face. "That we're not going to get our toe shoes?"

"Of course not," Zan replied. "We have the Amber Stone to make us better dancers." She patted the little wooden box gently.

"Right," McGee declared. "We don't have to worry about a thing."

The girls made one more hurried bow to the box. Then, with their shoulders back and chins held high, they marched proudly past the Bunheads into the studio.

Chapter Six

"All right, girls, gather around," Annie Springer called to the class. "I want to talk to you for a moment." The dark-haired ballerina waited patiently by the grand piano as her students clustered around her. The studio was charged with a special excitement and every girl's eyes seemed to shine more brightly than usual.

Annie looked out at them and smiled. She wore her usual uniform of a black vee-necked leotard with a short black nylon skirt encircling her waist. But today Annie had pinned a pink carnation to her hair, which made her seem lovelier than ever.

"I know how excited you all must be," she began.

A nervous giggle went around the room.

"The day a girl receives her toe shoes is a big event in every dancer's life," Annie continued. "And one you will never forget."

Suddenly the door to the ballet studio opened and Mr. Anton swept into the room. He was an elegant man, with a thick shock of silver hair and penetrating blue eyes. He wore a black turtleneck sweater and gray stretch dance pants.

The class instinctively moved to the ballet *barre* and stood at attention.

McGee nudged Rocky and asked, "What's that under his arm?"

Rocky squinted at the slim rectangular object Mr. Anton was carrying and shook her head. "I can't tell."

Gwen, however, had recognized it immediately but could only open and close her mouth in shock. Finally she choked out, "I — I can't believe it. This is too terrible for words."

"What is it?" McGee asked as Mr. Anton set the white-and-silver object on the floor.

Gwen fell back against the ballet *barre* in anguish. "It's a scale!"

"A scale?" Mary Bubnik looked perplexed. "What for?"

"To weigh us." Gwen could feel her heart pounding in her chest. "This is just awful," she groaned. "My mother didn't pay good money to have me die of embarrassment in front of a group of skinny girls." She looked around frantically. "I've got to get out of here."

"Hey, chill out, Gwen," Rocky said, grabbing her by the arm. "Let's wait to hear what he has to say."

"Good afternoon, ladies," the director said.

"Good afternoon, Mr. Anton," came the chorused reply.

"Today I will be talking with each of you." He clasped his hands behind his back and walked up and down the line of dancers. "First you will be weighed and then you will perform a series of exercises to determine the strength of your ankles and feet."

A low groan went around the room and Mr. Anton, who rarely smiled, laughed lightly. "I know it must sound like torture but it is quite painless. Ask your teacher."

"Mr. Anton's right," Annie said. "It should be a breeze. Just remember what I've taught you. Keep your shoulders back, your tummies tucked in, and feet turned out."

The class snapped to attention, as the girls threw back their shoulders, sucked in their stomachs, and strained to put their feet in fifth position.

"How long do we have to stay like this?" Gwen squeaked. She was holding her breath to keep her stomach from bulging out. "I already hurt."

"Until he gets to us," Rocky whispered back.

47

Rocky's shoulders were so far back her chin stuck out.

Miss Springer looked around the class and nodded at a slim brunette. "Tina, why don't you go first?" She pointed to the scale and grinned. "Step right up. It won't hurt a bit."

Tina smiled shyly and then stepped on the scale. "Eighty-three pounds," Mr. Anton read off in a loud voice while Annie wrote it down on the clipboard.

Gwen let out all of her air with a loud gasp. "Did you hear that? He's *broadcasting* our weight! He's blabbing it to the whole world!" She ran her hand through her short red hair. "I can't take this."

While Gwen writhed in silent agony, Mr. Anton put Tina through a series of steps, keeping a close watch on her ankles. When she was finished he patted her on the shoulder. "Nicely done, Tina. You have very strong feet and should do just fine *en pointe.*"

Tina flew back to her position at the *barre* and hugged her friends.

One by one the girls stepped forward, and soon it was Mary Bubnik's turn. As she stood on the scale Mr. Anton stared down at her feet and scratched his head. "Your shoes seem to be . . . a little large."

Mary giggled nervously. "My mother has this idea that I'll grow into them, but so far they just keep flapping around."

Mr. Anton cleared his throat. "Well, that could be

dangerous, young lady. If, and when, you do get toe shoes, they must fit snugly, like a second skin."

Mr. Anton read off her weight, and then had Mary *relevée* several times, raising up onto half *pointe.* Only once did she teeter dangerously but, with a high-pitched giggle, she regained her balance and finished the exercise.

Gwen, who was watching with the others, murmured, "I wish she'd quit laughing like that. Mary sounds like an idiot."

"She's just a little nervous," Zan whispered back. She was feeling a little shaky herself.

Finally Mr. Anton said, "I want you to do two things for me, Mary Bubnik. First, try to learn a little self-control, and second, you *must* get some shoes that fit."

Mary's lower lip quivered. "Does that mean I don't get my toe shoes?"

"Not at all," Mr. Anton said. "Your feet are strong enough. I see no reason why you shouldn't get your toe shoes."

"Oh, thank you!" Mary squealed. To Mr. Anton's surprise Mary threw her arms around him and hugged him tight. His steely blue eyes opened wide.

Then Mary skipped back over to her friends and shouted, "Can you believe it? I'm going to be a real ballerina!"

"Oh, puh-leeze!" Courtney groaned from the far side of the room.

Zan was next. She focused all of her attention on standing up straight and keeping her shoulders back. As she walked to the front of the class Zan realized that she was more scared now than she had been at the spelling bee.

But she needn't have worried. Mr. Anton assured her that she was ready for toe shoes, even adding, "You have the perfect body for a dancer. Long legs and arms — and such a nice long neck."

"Sounds more like a giraffe than a dancer," Alice Wescott snickered to her friends.

Beads of sweat were starting to prickle across Gwen's forehead. Of the gang, only McGee and Rocky were left before it was her turn. She needed to lose some weight fast.

Gwen had weighed in enough times at the doctor's office to know that shoes always added at least two pounds. She slipped out of her ballet slippers and shoved them into her dance bag. Then she removed her watch and the ring her grandmother had given her for her eleventh birthday. As an afterthought she took off her glasses. "These weigh a ton."

The room suddenly became a soft blur as she listened to Mr. Anton award Rocky her toe shoes.

"Oh, great!" Gwen mumbled to herself. "The biggest tomboy in the class just passed the ballerina test. I wonder if they make high-top toe shoes?"

Meanwhile Mr. Anton had focused his attention on McGee and was lecturing her sternly. "If you are to become a serious ballerina, you must take more care with your appearance." He pointed to a gaping hole in the knee of her tights.

For a second Gwen thought McGee might be flunked for slobbiness but then Mr. Anton added, "You have the legs of a true athlete. Just right for toe shoes."

"All right!" McGee shouted as she jogged back to the others, a lopsided grin plastered across her face.

Now it was Gwen's turn. She faced the blurry image of Mr. Anton, hoping for an earthquake or a flood to save her from the humiliation she knew was ahead.

Maybe I'll faint, or drop dead, Gwen thought hopefully. Then they'll be sorry.

An image flashed through her mind of Mr. Anton and the Bunheads sadly carrying her out of the studio. She imagined Miss Springer standing nearby, with tears in her eyes. "It was the weigh-in that got her," Annie would cry. "It was just too much for her heart."

McGee waved her hand in front of Gwen's face. "Earth to Gwen."

Gwen snapped back to the present as Rocky shoved her in the ribs. "You're up."

Gwen spun and hissed, "Don't push!"

"Gwendolyn Hays!" Mr. Anton snapped his fingers impatiently. "Please get on the scale."

His words were so commanding that she obeyed without hesitation.

"Hmmm," Mr. Anton murmured, studying the scale. "It seems you've been eating too many milk shakes and french fries after school." He poked his finger into the bulge around her waist and shook his head. "You will definitely have to do something about *that!*"

Now! a voice screamed inside Gwen's head. *Let me die now! Let lightning strike me right here! Let the earth open up and swallow me whole!*

But she had no such luck. Mr. Anton announced her weight to the whole class in the loudest voice possible. Gwen winced as she heard several gasps of shock. But the final blow came when Page Tuttle turned to Courtney and whispered, just loud enough for everyone to hear, "I knew she was fat, but I never dreamed she was *that* fat."

Gwen felt like her cheeks were on fire. She stumbled through the exercises Mr. Anton gave her, concentrating on one thing. Whatever you do, she told herself, don't cry.

Mr. Anton crossed his arms and walked in a circle around her, stroking his chin. "Your feet and legs are strong. Your coordination is quite good. But . . ." He shook his head. "I'm concerned about your weight, Gwendolyn. For now, I must say no to toe shoes."

Gwen hung her head in shame and turned to walk away.

"Just a moment," Mr. Anton said. "If you can show me you have the discipline to control your weight, I will reconsider my decision. The choice is yours. Miss Springer and I will check you again in a week or so."

Gwen barely heard what he was saying. She forced her legs to carry her back to the *barre* where she picked up her belongings and slipped her glasses onto her nose. Without looking to the left or the right, she walked up to Annie Springer and whispered, "May I please be excused? I don't feel well."

"Of course, Gwen," Annie said, her eyes warm with sympathy. "I understand."

Having her teacher feel sorry for her made Gwen feel even worse. If I can just make it out the door, she thought, I'll be fine.

A familiar voice pierced the air and her heart. "She'll never get her toe shoes," Courtney jeered. "She's just a blubberina!"

Hot tears filled Gwen's eyes as she stumbled out of the studio.

Chapter Seven

Gwen stared at her reflection in the window of the Polar Bear Ice Cream Parlor. A plump, freckle-faced girl with short red hair and glasses blinked back at her. "Courtney's right," she moaned. "You are a blubberina."

She stuck out her tongue at herself and then walked slowly down the street, pausing to stare in each store's window. She took a lick of her cone. Three scoops of doublenut fudge balanced on top of each other. Gwen had hoped the ice cream would make her feel better but it didn't. It just made her feel fat and miserable.

"Stupid old stone of Anastasia!" Gwen grumbled out loud. "It's nothing but a chipped rock." She felt in her pocket for the Twinkies and jumbo size pack of M&Ms that she had taken back in the dressing room. "I never really believed in it in the first place."

Gwen paused in front of Zimmerman's shoe store. They were the biggest supplier of dancewear in Deerfield. Several pairs of satin toe shoes were perched on a pedestal in the window, and Gwen looked longingly at them for several minutes.

"They're beautiful, aren't they?" a soft voice asked from beside her.

Gwen turned so fast she nearly dropped her ice-cream cone. A tiny brunette smiled shyly at her. Gwen recognized the girl as Julie McKenna from her ballet class.

Julie put one hand against the store's window and sighed, "All my life I've wanted to dance on toe shoes like a real ballerina."

Gwen finished off her cone with a loud crunch. "I guess you'll get your wish next week."

Julie shook her head sadly. "I'm on probation, too."

"What for?" Gwen choked. "You're a toothpick."

Julie stared down. "That's my problem."

"You mean, Mr. Anton has rules about being too skinny?" Gwen gasped. "I can't believe it. That guy is strict!"

Julie tucked a strand of her light brown hair behind one ear. "It's not just that. He thinks my feet aren't strong enough."

Gwen remembered the Twinkies in her pocket and pulled the pack out. "Have some of these, and they'll give you strength and put some weight on you." Then she grinned. "Just ask me. I'm an authority."

Julie giggled and took the cake Gwen had offered. "Thanks. They're one of my favorites."

As the girls ate their Twinkies, Julie said, "Getting my toe shoes is really important to me. I need to prove to them that I can do it."

Gwen didn't ask who *them* was. But she realized she had her own *them.* The Bunheads and kids who teased her about her weight at school.

The two girls looked back at the toe shoes in the window and sighed.

"Hey, Gwen!"

She looked up to see McGee standing on the corner at the end of the block. McGee cupped her hands around her mouth and shouted, "Where've you been? We've been looking all over for you."

"I needed some fresh air," Gwen called back. "So I took a walk. I feel much better now."

"Great!" McGee motioned for Gwen to join her. "The rest of the gang is waiting for us at Hi Lo's. Come on!"

"I, uh, have to go meet my friends," she explained to Julie as she polished her glasses on her parka. "I guess I'll see you next week."

Julie nodded. "I guess." As Gwen hurried down

56

the street she heard Julie call after her, "Good luck."

"Good luck to you, too!" Gwen shouted over her shoulder.

Gwen was almost to the corner when she suddenly felt a pang of guilt for not asking Julie to join them. She knew that misery loved company and decided to invite her. But when she turned around, the sidewalk in front of Zimmerman's shoe store was empty.

McGee stood in front of the tiny restaurant waiting for Gwen. The red-and-white sign hanging over the picture window read Hi Lo's Pizza and Chinese Food To Go.

"Look, Gwen," McGee said, adjusting her baseball cap. "I'm sorry about what happened today. I know you must feel rotten."

"Rotten?" Gwen repeated. "That's putting it mildly. I feel like someone punched me in the stomach, backed over me with a car, and then spit on me."

McGee wrinkled her nose. "That's gross."

Gwen shrugged. "That's the way I feel."

"Maybe one of Hi Lo's Super Dooper specials will make you feel better," McGee suggested.

"Maybe," Gwen said. "But I doubt it."

Hi Lo was the Chinese man who owned the little restaurant. He was their special friend and famous for the interesting ingredients he added to his milk shakes. Sometimes they tasted wonderful, like the time he put raspberry jam in a vanilla shake. And sometimes they were just strange, consisting of chunky peanut butter, marshmallows, and bananas in a chocolate swirl.

"Come on." McGee threw open the glass door and the little brass bell tinkled over their heads. The restaurant was tiny. One booth sat against the back wall and six round stools covered in torn and faded red leather lined the curved counter. Hi Lo was standing behind it, sharing a joke with Rocky, Zan, and Mary Bubnik.

"Hi, Hi!" McGee sang out in greeting.

Mr. Lo spotted the newcomers and his face creased into a thousand tiny wrinkles. "Greetings and salutations, my friends!" He patted the counter in front of him. "Have a seat. Or should I say, a stool." He winked and added, "I have something very special to offer you today."

"I hope it's not ice cream," Gwen said. The three scoops of chocolate ice cream and the Twinkies were starting to churn inside her stomach.

Hi laughed. "Oh, no. Today is Hawaiian Pizza day."

"Pizza?" Gwen raised an eyebrow. That happened to be her absolute favorite food. "Maybe a slice wouldn't hurt."

"I'll be right back." Hi disappeared into the kitchen.

Gwen sat down on the middle stool. The others looked at her carefully, trying to gauge her mood. Finally Mary Bubnik said, "I think I've figured out what went wrong with the Amber Stone of Anastasia."

"I'd rather not talk about that stupid old rock," Gwen grumbled.

"No, really, it's quite simple," Mary persisted. "You see, too many of us were using it at one time. It got overloaded."

"A rock got overloaded?" Gwen repeated skeptically. "I'm sure."

"Wait a minute," McGee said. "Maybe Mary's right. I mean, it seemed to be working just fine until five of us tried to use it."

Zan spun on her stool to face Gwen. "I used it to win the spelling bee."

"And it helped me get that terrific grade in geography," Mary Bubnik added.

"Yeah, that terrific C," Gwen said, rolling her eyes.

"Maybe four is the maximum number of people who can use it," Zan said thoughtfully.

"And because you were the last one to take the toe-shoe test," McGee added, "it didn't work for you."

"Gee, thanks," Gwen said sarcastically. "I feel a whole lot better, knowing I was singled out to be the only loser."

"I didn't mean it that way," McGee said, lightly punching Gwen on the shoulder.

"Here we are," Hi announced as he came through the swinging door from the kitchen. "The Hawaiian Pizza Special." He carried a circular tray that held the thickest pizza any of them had ever seen. The steam curled into the air and the girls inhaled the rich aroma.

"It truly smells delicious," Zan exclaimed. "Like cheese and ham."

"And tomatoes," Rocky added.

"And fresh pineapple," Mary Bubnik finished.

"Is that what makes it Hawaiian?" McGee asked as she tucked a napkin under her chin.

Hi Lo set the tray on the counter and beamed. "That and the coconut."

"Coconut?" Rocky cried, pushing her plate away from her. "Make me gag!"

"Have you ever had coconut on pizza before?" Hi asked: The girls shook their heads. "Then I suggest you try it before you reject it. It's always a big hit with my customers."

"That's why the place is so packed," Gwen murmured, looking around at the empty restaurant.

Hi raised a cautioning finger. "Never judge a pizza by its individual ingredients. Believe that it will be delicious, and it will be."

All of them gulped at once. Finally McGee shrugged. "I'm willing to try it if the rest of you are."

"It sure does smell good," Mary Bubnik said wistfully.

"I say we go for it," Rocky declared.

All five of them grabbed a slice of pizza at once. They sunk their teeth into the thick crust and a murmur of delight came from each of them. Hi wiped his hands on his apron in satisfaction and disappeared back into the kitchen. Behind the swinging door they could hear him chuckling, "I knew they'd like it."

Zan took another dainty bite of her pizza and set it on the napkin in front of her. "Hi said for us to believe that it's good, and it is. Maybe the same thing works for —" She lowered her voice. "The Amber Stone of Anastasia."

"What do you mean?" Rocky asked, twirling a long strand of cheese into her mouth.

"Maybe Gwen didn't believe in it enough," Mary Bubnik explained.

Gwen stuffed a huge piece of pizza in her mouth and mumbled, "I wish we'd just quit talking about it."

"I believe in it," McGee declared suddenly. "And I would like to ask permission to become the Keeper of the Stone for this coming week."

Zan set down her slice of pizza and put on her dramatic voice she used when talking about the sacred stone. "And for what high purpose do you need to use the powers of Anastasia?"

"We've got spring tryouts for Little League on Tuesday night." McGee shoved her cap back on her head and imitated Zan's tone of voice. "I need the Amber Stone of Anastasia to give me strength."

Zan and Mary Bubnik put their heads together for a moment and conferred. Then they nodded and

Mary Bubnik, who had been keeping the box in front of her on the counter, carefully handed it to McGee. "I give to you the sacred stone. Protect it with your life, and believe in it with your heart." She bowed and McGee bowed back.

"Thanks, guys," McGee replied in her normal voice. "I've been in training for weeks, working on my throw and my swing, but I need all the help I can get. I really want to be the catcher for the Bombers. They're the hottest team in Fairview."

"Training!" Rocky pounded her fist on the counter so hard that everyone jumped. "That's the answer."

"I missed something." Gwen shoved her glasses up on her nose. "The answer to what?"

"Your problem," Rocky explained. "You need to go into training."

"I do?"

"Geez Louise!" McGee hit her forehead with the palm of her hand. "Why didn't I think of that? I'll be your personal trainer. We can work out together."

"And Zan and Rocky and I can be your assistants," Mary Bubnik cried out with glee.

"I've read about personal trainers," Zan said excitedly. "Everyone in Hollywood has one. Movie stars, rock singers — that's how they always look so great."

Gwen squinted at McGee. "You mean running and jumping and sweating?"

"Maybe she should pump some iron, too," Rocky suggested.

"What?" Gwen cried out in alarm.

"Lift weights," McGee explained quickly.

"I could bring some of my brothers' stuff. They've got plenty to spare." Rocky had four brothers and with all of their equipment, her mother often said their house looked more like a gym than a home.

"Great idea," McGee said enthusiastically. "We'll start with some ankle weights to strengthen your legs. Then get some dumbbells and really focus in on waist benders." She poked a finger at Gwen's bulging waist.

"Now, hold on a minute," Gwen said, nearly falling off her stool. "I'm not really the athletic type, you know. I prefer to read and play the piano."

"Then it's settled." McGee clapped her hands together. "We can work out at Glenwood Park. They have a great track and a big field, too."

"We'll start tomorrow," Mary Bubnik announced.

"I don't know," Gwen said hesitantly. "I've got to think about this." She was reaching for the last slice of pizza on the tray when Rocky grabbed her arm.

"I don't think we should wait till tomorrow," Rocky said.

"What do you mean?" Gwen asked, struggling to free her arm.

"I think you should start right now," Rocky replied. "With exercise number one — pushing yourself away from the table."

Chapter Eight

Just after sunup on Sunday morning McGee pulled on her blue warm-up suit and baseball cap, and looped a whistle around her neck. She hopped on her ten speed and pedaled as hard as she could toward Gwen's house in Brooke Hollow.

As she rode through the housing development McGee spotted people in their bathrobes picking up their Sunday papers. A roly-poly dachshund chased her up Gwen's street all the way from the corner. By the time she pulled into the driveway of the Hays' ranch-style home, she was completely out of breath. McGee wheeled her bike up to the door and rang the bell.

The drapes were still drawn and it took another

ring and several more minutes before she heard the lock click open. Finally the big white door swung open and a strange figure dressed in pink squinted out at her.

"Kathryn?" a hoarse voice croaked. "Is that you?"

McGee couldn't believe her eyes. She had never seen Gwen's mother without makeup. The tall blonde woman had been a model when she was younger and always looked exquisite. Even this morning Mrs. Hays was clad in pink silk pajamas and a flowing chiffon robe with matching satin slippers. But there were big dark circles under her eyes and a pink satin sleeping mask perched crookedly on top of her tousled hair.

Mrs. Hays shielded her eyes from the glare of the sun and asked, "What's the matter? Has something happened to your mother?"

McGee shook her head. "Mom's fine. I'm here to get Gwen."

"Now?" The woman squinted at the wall clock hanging in the hall. "But it's still the middle of the night."

"It's nearly eight o'clock, Mrs. Hays," McGee said slowly. "My family's already had breakfast, and Mom's busy painting the back porch."

"She's setting a bad example for the rest of us," Mrs. Hays replied, stifling a yawn. She and Mrs. McGee were best friends, but as different as night and day. McGee figured that's why they liked each other.

"The reason I'm here so early," McGee explained,

"is because Gwen is starting a workout program this morning."

"*My* daughter?" Mrs. Hays's eyes widened for a second. "I don't believe it."

"It's true." McGee shifted from one foot to the other impatiently. "Just ask her."

Mrs. Hays opened the door a little wider and gestured for McGee to come inside. "I'll see if she's up." McGee stepped through the door and perched on the white couch in the living room. She heard Mrs. Hays's slippers shuffle down the hall and then her voice call, "Gwendolyn? Are you awake?"

There came a loud groan, followed by a voice muttering, "Go away."

"Gwendolyn Hays?" Her mother rapped on the bedroom door. "Get up this minute. You have company."

"But it's Sunday," came the muffled reply. "We always sleep in on Sunday."

"That's what *I* thought," her mother replied in an exaggeratedly sweet tone, "but apparently you invited a friend to come sound the wake-up gong." Her voice hardened and she snapped, "Now I want you out of that bed this instant!"

Mrs. Hays padded back into the living room and smiled stiffly. "Excuse me, but I'm not alive yet. I need my morning coffee." She groped her way toward the kitchen and McGee listened to the sound of water running and glass clinking.

Moments later Gwen shuffled into the room. She was the complete opposite of her mother. Instead of pink satin pajamas she wore a pair of old gray sweatpants and a Mickey Mouse T-shirt. Mickey's face had faded and been replaced by several large stains that looked suspiciously like ketchup and chocolate. But what really caught McGee's attention were her slippers. They were fuzzy fluorescent green rabbits with floppy ears. The one on her right foot was missing an ear and both eyes had fallen out of the left one.

"Oh. It's you," Gwen said lifelessly.

Mrs. Hays stuck her head into the living room. "McGee says you're starting a workout program this morning."

Gwen squinted at her mother. "McGee's a liar." Then she turned and shuffled back toward her bedroom. McGee was off the couch in a flash.

"Oh, no, you don't!" She grabbed Gwen by the elbow and spun her around. "Training starts at nine o'clock in Glenwood Park."

"Well, it will have to start without this girl," Gwen croaked. "I need my beauty sleep."

"Not so fast." McGee pulled Gwen into the bathroom and splashed water on her face. "Wake up. This is an important day. Everyone's waiting for you."

Gwen's straight red hair had a big fuzzy knot in the back of it and she made a half-hearted attempt to smooth it out. "I can't go anywhere looking like this."

"Wear a hat!" McGee slammed her own baseball cap on top of Gwen's head. "Now come on."

A few minutes later the girls were pedaling on their bikes toward Glenwood Park.

"The least you could have done was let me eat breakfast," Gwen complained.

"I did."

"A bowl of cereal and a measly piece of toast? That's not breakfast — that's a snack."

"Under your new training program, that's all you get." McGee set her jaw firmly. "And I'm thinking of cutting out the toast."

"Over my dead body," Gwen grumbled as she followed McGee down the side roads.

"We'll be right on time," McGee shouted, checking her watch. "If we pick up the pace a little."

Gwen strained forward over the handle bars and struggled to catch up with McGee. "You know," she huffed as she rolled up beside her, "my mother will never forgive you."

"Why? For getting you up early?"

"No. For seeing her without her makeup."

The girls pedaled the rest of the way in silence. By the time they reached the entrance of the huge park, sweat was already dripping down Gwen's forehead into her eyes. She dabbed at her face with the sleeve of her sweatshirt and asked, "Where are we meeting, anyway?"

"At the circuit run," McGee shouted.

"What's that?"

"It's like an obstacle course. You'll see, it's lots of fun."

"I can't wait."

They parked their bikes in the bike stand and then McGee led Gwen up the sidewalk to the start of the course.

Three strangely dressed figures were there waiting for them.

"They look like rejects from an aerobics class," Gwen muttered under her breath.

Rocky was dressed in cut-offs and a black T-shirt that read Metal Rules! She had the sleeves of her red satin jacket pushed up onto her forearms, and she wore a new pair of sunglasses on her nose.

Mary had stuffed her bouncy curls inside a man's golf cap that was too large for her and was wearing a shocking pink warm-up suit.

Zan wore a crisp white polo shirt with a pair of baggy tan shorts and new tennis shoes. A green sports visor shaded her eyes and she held a clip-board in her hands.

"Let's get this show on the road," McGee declared, dropping her blue canvas knapsack on the ground. She pulled out a small cassette player and turned it on full. Then she grabbed the whistle and let out a shrill blast. "Time for warm-ups. Everybody line up in front of me."

Rocky and Mary grabbed Gwen by each arm and stood her between them, facing McGee, who arched over to the side and shouted, "And strrrr-e-tch!"

For ten minutes McGee ran them through a brisk series of jumping jacks, side stretches, calf pulls, and knee bends, counting to four the whole time. Just when Gwen would get the hang of one exercise, McGee would change to another.

Finally Gwen snapped, "Look, just make up your mind, will you? Why do we have to go so fast, anyway?"

"To get your heart rate up," McGee explained.

"If it goes any higher, I'll have a heart attack."

The tape ran out and Gwen bent over to catch her breath. The others were breathing hard, too. Finally Gwen straightened up and announced brightly, "Well, that was great. Thanks a lot, guys. I feel at least ten pounds lighter." As she spoke she backed toward the sidewalk.

"Where are you going?" McGee demanded.

"Aren't we finished?" Gwen asked.

"That was just the warm-up. Your workout's only begun."

"That's right," Zan agreed. "You still have to do your sit-ups."

"And the circuit run," Mary Bubnik added.

"No thanks," Gwen said with a laugh. "I think I'll just coast on home and watch a ballgame on TV.

You see, those people get *paid* to do this sort of thing —"

"OK, Rocky," McGee interrupted. "Take over."

Rocky faced Gwen and shouted in her best drill sergeant's voice, "Ten-*hut!*" Without thinking, Gwen snapped to attention. Rocky shoved her face up close to Gwen's and roared, "All right! You're gonna do the circuit run, and you're gonna do it *hard!* Now march! *One*-two-three-four!"

What happened next seemed to Gwen to be something out of a nightmare. First they made her lay down on a slanting board and do fifty sit-ups. Gwen made it through the first three but Rocky and Mary Bubnik had to shove her forward and back to finish the rest.

Then she had to run down a row of old tires, stepping in and out of each one. The edges of the tires caught her ankles and tripped her three or four times but the others ran alongside, shouting encouragement, until finally Gwen emerged triumphant at the other end.

The wall posed the first big problem. Rocky demonstrated how she was supposed to get a running start at it, then hook her hands over the top and swing the rest of her body over to the other side of the wall.

The first time Gwen tried it, she forgot to jump up and ran full force into the wall, knocking the wind out of her. The next time, she hooked her hands over the top but couldn't swing over. She just hung helplessly by her arms. Finally Rocky and McGee got beneath her and with a mighty heave shoved her over the top.

"Good job," McGee declared. "All that's left is the rope climb."

They half-carried, half-dragged Gwen over to a trestle that had several thick ropes hanging down to the ground beneath it. Each rope was about fifteen feet long. Gwen took one look and shook her head. "Absolutely not."

"It's easier than it looks," McGee explained. "You wrap your legs around it like this—" She grabbed the nearest rope to demonstrate and shinnied easily up to the top. "And then you just pull yourself up and ring the bell." A little bell hung at the summit of each climb and McGee rang hers, then slid back down to the ground. "Easy."

Gwen held her ground. "That's easy for you. You're an athlete. I'm not going to do it unless everybody does it."

McGee shrugged. "That's only fair. Coach says you should never ask someone to do something you wouldn't do yourself."

Rocky went first. She shinnied up and down the rope almost as quickly as McGee. Zan struggled a bit but made it to the top and proudly rang the bell. "I did it!"

Then it was Mary Bubnik's turn. She got halfway

up when somehow the rope got twisted and she flipped upside down. "Help!"

"Don't panic, Mary," Zan cried as the others all rushed forward. "We'll get you down."

"I don't know where I am," Mary Bubnik screamed. "Everything's topsy-turvy."

"Just use your feet to slide back down," Rocky instructed, positioning herself beneath Mary Bubnik.

"Whatever you do," McGee warned, "don't let go of the rope."

"Let go of the rope?" Mary shouted. "OK."

Fortunately for Mary, Rocky was standing right beneath her and broke her fall. But the force of the fall knocked Rocky flat on her face in the dirt. They lay in a tangle of legs and arms.

"Are you OK, Mary?" Zan asked as she and McGee helped her to her feet.

"Oh, shucks, I'm fine," Mary giggled. "I never felt a thing."

"I did," Rocky groaned, gingerly probing her side with her hand as she stood up. "I think you broke my back."

Meanwhile Gwen had been lying under a tree, watching the entire episode. "Hey, guys, let's call it a day on the old circuit run, OK?"

McGee looked at Rocky, who nodded. "I have to catch the bus back to the base pretty soon anyway." She crossed her eyes and added, "My dad's planned one of his family outings."

The gang staggered out of the woods onto a little knoll near the playground.

"Water!" Gwen gasped as she dropped face first onto the cool grass. "I'm dying of thirst."

"Me, too," Zan agreed as they all sprawled out beside Gwen on the ground.

"I wish there was a refreshment stand or something," Mary Bubnik drawled. "I'd give anything for an ice cold soda."

Gwen raised up on her elbows and surveyed the grassy expanse of park. "Hey! I think there may be something like that on the other side of the softball field."

Rocky sat up abruptly. "Where?"

"Over there with the striped awning," McGee replied.

Rocky leaped to her feet and shouted, "Last one there is a rotten..." Her words died in her throat. "Oh, no."

"What's the matter?" Zan asked.

Rocky didn't answer but flattened herself out on the ground.

"What is it?" Mary Bubnik asked. "What'd she see?"

"I don't know." Gwen turned slowly in a circle. "All I see is a family with a stroller, two old men with straw hats, and four boys in jean jackets."

"Hide me!" Rocky moaned, raising her head to peek at the boys. "It's Russell Stokes." At the same moment the tallest of the four spotted her and pointed with his finger. "There she is! Get her!"

Rocky looked frantically for someplace to hide but there was no escape. She leaped to her feet and, crouching in her karate pose of self-defense, screamed, "One step closer and the four of you are hamburger."

Her words sounded tough, but the girls could hear the fear in her voice. The tall boy put his hands on his hips and laughed. "Oh, yeah? Who's doing the cooking?"

Rocky gestured to her friends, who huddled tightly around her. "My gang. They've all been trained in karate and I wouldn't risk tangling with them."

Gwen tried to suck in her stomach and get a vicious look on her face. McGee pushed up the sleeves of her sweatsuit as Zan and Mary Bubnik made growling sounds.

"They don't look so tough," one of the other boys said.

"Oh, yeah?" McGee snapped. "Want to find out?"

The tall boy held his ground. "Look, I don't want to mess with anyone but Garcia." He stared at Rocky and snapped, "Now give it back."

"What?" she retorted.

"You know what."

"I have no idea what you're talking about."

One of the boys noticed the blue knapsack Rocky was carrying and nudged Russell. "I'll bet she's got it in that bag."

The boys lunged for Rocky just as the city bus rounded the corner. "Throw me the bag," McGee shouted.

Rocky tossed it over one of the shorter boy's head and McGee caught it. The boys immediately turned on her.

"Rocky," Zan hissed, "your bus is here. Run for it!"

The brakes of the bus squealed as it pulled to a stop and Rocky bolted for the door. McGee was glad she'd been in training because she was easily able to outdistance the boys — even Russell Stokes.

Rocky leaped on the bus and raced to the back seat where she opened the window. "McGee! My bag!"

McGee leaped for the curb and tossed the bag up in the air. For a moment it looked like it would fly over the roof of the bus but Rocky leaned out the window and snagged it with one hand.

"Two points!" McGee shouted, raising her arms in triumph.

Then Rocky's voice echoed tauntingly from the bus as it pulled away from the curb. "Missed me, missed me, now you've got to kiss me."

The boys turned and ran down the street after the bus, shaking their fists.

Mary Bubnik turned to her three friends and asked, "What do we do now?"

"Well, in light of what's happened," Gwen said, calmly pushing her glasses up on her nose, "I suggest we run for it while we can still walk."

Chapter Nine

"McGee's going to have some real competition," Gwen declared as the girls took their seats on the top row of bleachers at Fairview's baseball field on Tuesday. "There must be two hundred kids here."

"It's not that bad." Rocky stood up and scanned the crowd for McGee. "They're trying out for a lot of teams, not just one."

"But I thought McGee only wanted to be on the Bombers," Mary Bubnik said, peering nervously down through the wooden slats. It made her dizzy being so high above the ground. Suddenly the wooden board she sat on bounced up and down. "It's an earthquake!"

"No, it's not," Gwen said as she clutched the seat

with her hands. "It's just Rocky, jumping up and down like a jerk. I think she's found McGee."

"She's over by the visitors dugout," Rocky shouted. "Come on. We need to hold a *you-know-what* before the tryouts start." Rocky wiggled her eyebrows and lowered her voice when she spoke but it wasn't really necessary. They all knew what "you-know-what" meant.

"The Sacred Ceremony of the Amber Stone," Mary Bubnik whispered.

"Leave something to save our place." Zan took off her cape and spread it carefully on the top row. The others removed their jackets and scarves and lay them out along the bleacher, then followed Rocky to the dugout.

McGee stood inside the chain link fence, doing stretching exercises. She wore a pair of bright red sweatpants and a baseball jersey that said Cincinnati Reds. Her catcher's mitt lay on the ground beside her.

"I'm glad you guys made it," McGee called through the fence. She reached for the sky and then bent over in little tiny bounces, putting the palms of her hands flat on the ground. "I'm just finishing my warm-up."

Mary Bubnik winced just watching her. "That must really hurt."

"It's a good kind of hurt," McGee said. "Although I am a little sore after yesterday's training session."

"I'm glad to hear you say that," Gwen said. " 'Cause I can barely walk. Just climbing up and down those bleachers nearly did me in."

"Good!" McGee grinned. "That means the exercises are working."

"They're working, all right." Gwen massaged her calf with her knuckles. "A few more sessions like that, and I won't have to worry about toe shoes. I won't even have to worry about shoes — I'll be in a wheelchair."

A whistle sounded and a man in a jogging suit and baseball cap trotted out to the pitcher's mound.

"Oh, no!" Mary Bubnik gasped. "The tryouts are starting, and we haven't done the sacred ceremony."

McGee scooped up her glove and the box. "Meet me at the backstop," she called through the fence. "I can't keep the box down here. You'll have to hold it for me."

The gang jogged along the chain link fence to the opening by the batter's cage. Zan took the box from McGee and hurriedly whispered, "Everyone, put your hand on the box."

They did as they were told. "Now repeat after me." She shut her eyes and intoned, "Oh, Amber Stone of Anastasia."

Gwen repeated the words with the others but kept sneaking little glances over her shoulders to make sure no one was watching them.

"Hear our plea." Keeping her eyes closed Zan

tilted her chin toward the sky. "Help McGee do her best today so she will be chosen by the Boomers —"

"It's the Bombers," McGee hissed.

Zan opened one eye. "Sorry." Then she closed it again and added, "Correction, Anastasia. She wants to be on the Bombers."

The whistle blew again so Zan sped up the ritual. "Because she believes in you with all her heart," she rattled off, "and will protect you with her life." Then she opened her eyes and whispered, "OK, everybody, bow three times. And hurry!"

Out on the field the man on the pitcher's mound introduced himself as the president of the Little League Association. Then he described how the tryouts would be run. By the time the gang made it back to their seats, the stands were packed with families with little kids and coolers full of soda pop.

"Could I hold the —?" Mary Bubnik lowered her voice to a whisper. "Could I hold the sacred stone for McGee?" Mary Bubnik had an ulterior motive for being the temporary Keeper. She figured it just might give her a little extra protection against falling off of the bleachers.

All the kids trying out for the different teams were divided into five groups — fielding, running, catching, batting, and pitching. The very first boy at bat hit a ball that popped up and over the backstop.

"Heads up!" someone in the crowd shouted.

"I got it!" Rocky leaped to her feet and nabbed

the ball with the tips of her fingers, nearly falling backwards over the guardrail. Mary Bubnik shut her eyes and clung to the bleacher for dear life.

"Nice catch," a voice called from the ground below.

A handsome boy with sun-streaked hair stood grinning up at her, his hands tucked in the pockets of his stone-washed denim jacket. Rocky tossed the ball back onto the field, then leaned over the railing and smiled. "Thanks."

Gwen peered over her shoulder to see what was going on. When she spotted the boy she whispered, "That guy is a mega-hunk."

"No kidding," Zan declared softly, joining them at the railing.

Mary Bubnik opened her eyes cautiously and peeked down at the ground. "Oooh, I think he's cute," she squealed.

"Shhh!" Rocky, Gwen, and Zan turned and hissed at once. "He'll hear you."

"No, he won't." Mary pointed to the brick building where refreshments were sold. "I think he's going to get something to eat."

The four girls watched the boy disappear around the corner and then reluctantly turned their attention back to the baseball diamond. They watched in silence as the different groups rotated around the field.

The fielders shifted to base running. The pitchers and catchers went up to bat and those at bat took the field. They searched for McGee's baseball cap and jersey but all of the kids seemed to look alike. It was hard for the girls to concentrate — they couldn't get that cute boy out of their minds.

Suddenly Rocky stood up and stretched. "I think I'll get a drink of water." She held out her hand to Mary Bubnik. "Give me the box, will you?"

Mary clutched it tightly to her chest. "What for?"

Rocky rolled her eyes. "I'm going closer to the field. It will bring McGee more luck that way. OK?"

Mary Bubnik hesitated and Gwen jumped in. "Look, I have to go to the bathroom," she said reasonably. "They're right next to the dugouts. Why don't I take the box?"

"I've got a better idea," Zan said. "McGee is doing batting now. I'll just take the box up to the backstop. I think that would work the best."

As Zan bent down for the box, Mary jerked it out of her reach and narrowed her eyes. "I think you guys just want it so you can meet that boy."

"What?" they all shouted indignantly.

"That's truly ridiculous!" Zan sniffed.

"I wouldn't dream of doing such a thing," Gwen said.

"Well, I would," Rocky barked. "Give me that!"

"Oh, no, you don't!" Gwen grabbed Rocky's arm and they fell back against the rail. "I want the box."

"Be careful," Mary Bubnik warned, "you're going to get hurt."

"Why don't you just give me the box?" Zan said slyly. "Then they won't have anything to fight about."

Rocky and Gwen recovered their balance just in time to see Zan make her move. They dove at Mary Bubnik and in the struggle the box suddenly tilted upside down.

"Look out!" Gwen watched in horror as the lid flipped open and the stone flew up into the air. It seemed to move in slow motion as it tumbled over and over and clattered down through the bleachers to the ground below.

Zan put her hands to her face in dismay. "You dropped the sacred stone!"

"*I* dropped it?" Mary Bubnik's lip began to quiver. "Y'all knocked it right out of my hands."

"I hope it's not bad luck," Rocky groaned.

They looked out at home plate just as McGee stepped into the batter's box. She swung hard at the first pitch and completely missed.

The girls gasped out loud. "We've got to find that stone," Rocky shouted, "before McGee strikes out."

They scrambled through the crowd on the bleachers down to the ground. Gwen was so upset she didn't even notice how much her muscles hurt as she leaped over the legs of startled spectators. They had to retrieve the stone before anything really terrible happened!

The girls ducked under the metal gridwork supporting the bleachers. When they found the area just beneath their seats, Rocky dropped down on her hands and knees and pawed through the discarded candy wrappers and popcorn boxes littering the ground.

"Yuck! This is too gross for words." Rocky raised her hand and a huge wad of pink bubble gum dangled from her palm.

"Be careful." Gwen gingerly poked the debris with a stick. "You might get some awful disease from touching that kind of trash."

"I found a penny!" Mary Bubnik called out.

"You better hope it's lucky and will help us find the stone," Rocky muttered. "'Cause this looks hopeless. There's too much junk to sift through."

Zan methodically crawled in a straight line beneath the seats, first one way, then another. "Can anyone see how McGee's doing?"

"I'm afraid to look," Mary Bubnik groaned.

"What're you looking for?" a male voice asked.

Rocky stood up so fast she banged her head on one of the metal braces. She rubbed the spot with her hand but didn't feel a thing. She was too busy looking into the sparkling blue eyes of the boy in the denim jacket. "Um . . . my friends and I dropped a, uh, stone."

"Oh it's not just any stone," Mary Bubnik blurted without thinking. "It's the Amber Stone of Anastasia."

Rocky and Gwen exchanged looks of horror. The

last thing they needed was to look like a bunch of airheads in front of a cool boy.

"Ha, ha!" Gwen forced a laugh. "She's always making things up like that."

"I am not," Mary Bubnik protested.

Zan stepped forward and explained in her shy voice, "You see, we're looking for a good luck charm that belongs to our friend." She pointed to Mary Bubnik. "Unfortunately — she dropped it."

"I did not!" Mary Bubnik cried indignantly.

"Anyway," Gwen cut in, "it's down here somewhere, and we need to find it before the little league tryouts are over."

The boy glanced out at the field "You'd better hurry. It looks like the head coach is giving the final talk."

"You're kidding!" Rocky leaped up and hit her head on the metal brace a second time. "Ow!" she shouted in pain. "This is terrible. McGee will never forgive us."

"I'll help you look for it," the blond-haired boy offered. "Just tell me what it looks like."

"It looks like a big drop of honey that's been turned to a beautiful amber stone," Mary Bubnik explained. "It's easy to spot because of the gash the Russian bullet made in the center."

"Russian bullet?" the boy asked. "You mean, someone shot at it?"

"They didn't actually shoot at the stone," Gwen tried to explain, all the while nudging Mary with her elbow to keep her quiet. "They fired at the girl who was wearing it."

"The stone stopped the bullet and saved her life," Zan finished.

Instead of thinking the girls were talking like idiots, the boy seemed very impressed. He dropped to his knees beside Rocky and started rummaging through the litter. "I'll find it for you."

"Great," Rocky said with a grin.

A thunderous noise sounded above their heads as all of the spectators stood up at once and jostled their way to the ground.

"We're going to be crushed," Mary Bubnik cried. "The whole thing's going to collapse, and we'll be flattened like a pizza."

"Uh-oh," Zan whispered suddenly. "McGee's coming this way."

"Does she look happy?" Rocky asked.

"It's hard to tell."

"Oh, no," Mary Bubnik moaned. "What if she struck out and didn't make the team just because we lost the Sacred Stone of Anastasia?"

"Is this it?" The cute boy held up the amber stone, and it flashed in the afternoon light.

"Yea!" Mary Bubnik squealed.

"Willard!"

The blond boy spun around and yelled, "What, Ma?"

Gwen and Rocky exchanged looks and silently mouthed, "Willard?"

A huge woman with four tiny children clinging to her dress was standing near the edge of the parking lot. "Get in the car this instant."

Willard smiled sheepishly at the girls. "Gotta run." He turned and trotted off toward the parking lot.

"Wait!" Rocky yelled. "The stone — fork it over."

Without looking back he tossed it over his shoulder and Rocky caught it with one hand.

"Can you believe that guy?" Rocky shook her head. "He was going to steal our lucky stone!"

"I believe it!" Mary Bubnik said, snatching it from Rocky's hand and depositing it in the box. "He knows what power it has."

"Let's just hope it didn't get angry," Zan said.

"Who was that?" McGee asked, joining them.

The girls looked guiltily at each other, and then Mary Bubnik said, "Just some boy who wanted to know what time it was."

"Yo, McGee," Rocky cut in. "How'd you do?"

All four of them held their breath.

"I made the cut," McGee said with a smile. "But I'm not sure I made the Bombers." She took the wooden box out of Mary's hands and patted it. "I wonder if the Amber Stone of Anastasia helped me hit that home run?"

The four girls looked at McGee in shock as Gwen patted her confidently on the back. "I'm sure it did."

Chapter Ten

On Wednesday afternoon Rocky rode the bus from the Air Force Base to Zan's house in downtown Deerfield. The gang had agreed to meet there for Part Two of Gwen's training program. Zan, who had read a lot of magazines about health spas, had volunteered to turn her family's apartment into a makeshift gym for the occasion.

Rocky carried a blue nylon backpack with several of her brothers' dumbbells inside. The bag felt like it weighed a ton. When she got off at Zan's stop, she walked a block and then paused to switch the backpack to her other shoulder. That's when she heard the footsteps clicking along behind her.

They stopped when she stopped. Rocky held her breath, afraid to turn around.

"Russell," she murmured out loud. "How could he have followed me here?"

Russell Stokes lived on the base, too. He must have followed her onto the bus and hid in the back. Rocky stepped up her pace, her red high-tops making little slapping sounds as she jogged down the street. Behind her she could hear the faint sound of another pair of running feet.

Her throat felt tight with fear. To calm herself she went over the directions to Zan's house again in her mind. "Two blocks from the bus stop on Allison Street. Turn right on Bellevue, left on High Street, and you're there."

At Bellevue Rocky made a sharp right. As she turned the corner she saw a figure out of the corner of her eye a hundred yards behind her. "If he follows me around the turn, then it's Russell for sure," she muttered to herself, pulling up in a doorway a few yards from the corner.

The footsteps paused at the corner, then moved in her direction. Rocky fled down the street, not daring to look back. She decided it was time to use "evasive tactics," as her father the sergeant would say.

Instead of turning left on High Street, like Zan had told her, Rocky went one block further and ducked into the first alley she passed. Then she ran with all her might past the garbage cans and fire escapes until she came to a narrow gap between the houses. On the other side of the street she could see the brick walls of Zan's apartment building.

Rocky stopped to catch her breath. Her chest ached and a sharp pain jabbed into her side. "I wish I hadn't brought these stupid weights." Rocky shifted the heavy bag to her other shoulder, then closed her eyes and listened hard. Her breathing was the only sound in the alley. Rocky counted to three, then whispered, "Run for it!"

She zigzagged between the houses, leaped over a tricycle and crawled on her hands and knees under a hedge. She burst into the daylight and pounded across the tree-lined street toward the entrance to Zan's apartment building.

"Lost him!" she said to herself as she bounded up the steps. "All right!" With a smile Rocky reached for the doorbell just as a hand grabbed hold of her shoulder.

"Haaaaiiiiieeeee!" Rocky screamed her best karate yell and spun around in a defensive posture.

"Wait, don't chop! It's me!"

Mary Bubnik tripped backwards down the steps and sat down hard on the sidewalk.

Rocky remained in her crouched position. "Mary," she demanded, "what are you doing here?"

"The same thing you are," Mary Bubnik replied. "I'm here to help Gwen get in shape."

Rocky crept to the edge of the porch and peered around one of the stone pillars of the old building. "Was there anyone with you when you came down the street?"

"No. I've been trying to catch up with you ever since you got off the bus." Mary got to her feet and brushed off her jeans. "Boy, you sure do run fast!"

Rocky looked stunned. "That was you?"

Mary nodded.

"There wasn't anyone nearby? A tall, dark-haired boy, about twelve, with a mean look on his face?"

"Nope, the street was empty except for you, running around like a chicken with its head cut off."

"Well, my dad always says, keep moving, you're harder to hit."

"But who'd want to hit you?" Mary asked. Then her eyes widened and she nodded. "I get it. That boy in the park the other day."

"Russell Stokes." Rocky ran her hand through her hair. "He's driving me crazy. He follows me to school. I can't go out to recess anymore. I have to have my older brothers walk me home."

"But why?" Mary asked. "How'd this whole fight with him get started?"

"Russell said I took his math book."

"Did you?"

"Yes." Rocky shoved her hands in her red satin jacket. "But not on purpose. You see, at recess last week, he tossed his books on top of mine while I was playing tetherball. When I went to get my stuff, his math book had fallen into my bag."

"Didn't you see it there?"

"Yeah, but I thought it was mine."

Mary frowned. "Where was your book?"

"Back in my locker. But I didn't know it then. Russell accused me of stealing, and I told him he was a dirty, rotten liar."

"Then what happened?" Mary Bubnik sat on the top step and looked up at Rocky.

"I hit him."

"What'd he do?"

"Hit me back — harder," Rocky said, tossing her wild mane of hair defiantly. "So then I took *all* of his books."

"His homework and everything?" Mary Bubnik blinked her big blue eyes in astonishment.

Rocky chuckled. "Yeah. Now he's in big trouble with the teachers."

"But I don't understand. If you really did take his book, why don't you just give it back to him?"

"I can't." Rocky pressed the doorbell for Zan's apartment. "If I give it back, he'll think I really did steal it."

"Couldn't you just explain what happened in a polite sort of way?"

"Polite?" Rocky snorted. "Russell Stokes doesn't know the meaning of the word. Remember, he's the one who broke my sunglasses the night of the spelling bee."

"Boy, that is a problem," Mary sighed.

"Hey, don't worry about me," Rocky declared. "I can handle it." She jumped to her feet and pressed the button next to the Reed's nameplate.

Suddenly a voice came over the intercom. "Who is it?"

"Hi, Zan," Rocky said, "it's us."

"Us who?" Zan's voice asked with a giggle.

Mary Bubnik joined Rocky at the intercom, and they both shouted, "Us Bubnik and Garcia."

Zan giggled again. "When you hear the buzzer, push open the door and come up to the third floor. I'll meet you in the hall."

The intercom clicked off, the door buzzed, and they hurried through the brightly lit lobby toward the stairs. As they passed the first floor landing, Mary snapped her fingers and announced, "I've decided that you need some extra help."

"You mean, like hire a gang to fight Russell's gang?"

"No, that wouldn't solve anything. What you need is *special* help." Mary had a mysterious smile on her face.

"You mean —?"

Mary nodded. "The Amber Stone of Anastasia."

Rocky hesitated on the stairs. "I don't know."

"It worked for McGee, Zan, and me," Mary reminded her. "I just know it'll work for you. We'll make you the official Keeper of the Stone. Take it home with you today, and I promise everything will work out just fine with mean old Russell Stokes."

Zan was waiting for them when they reached the third floor. She was dressed in a white painter's smock and her green visor. "Welcome to Madame Zan's Fit 'n' Trim Health Spa."

"Where'd you get that coat?" Rocky asked. "You look like a doctor."

"My mom wears these when she sculpts," Zan explained. "It looks exactly like the staff uniforms at those fancy weight loss clinics in Switzerland. I saw a picture in a travel magazine."

"Oooh, I want to wear one, too!" Mary Bubnik cried.

"Come on in," Zan replied. "I'll get you both one."

Zan led them into the living room. The Reed apartment was an open loft that took up the entire third floor. Both of Zan's parents were artists and taught at the Deerfield Art Institute. They had decorated their house in an ultra modern style, with chrome and glass furnishings and thick white carpet everywhere. Every wall was covered with colorful woven hangings and paintings, with unique sculptures set in the corners.

"Mom and Dad are at the Institute today so we have the entire house to ourselves," Zan said. The doorbell rang and she hurried over to a little console by the front door.

"Madame Zan's Fit 'n' Trim Health Spa," Zan spoke into the intercom in an adult-sounding voice. "Who is it?"

When Zan pushed the button marked Listen, they heard McGee's voice shout, "It's McGee and Gwen. Let us in."

"Madame Zan is ready to receive you." Then she switched back to her normal voice. "Hurry up! We don't have much time."

While they waited for the girls, Zan passed out white smocks to Rocky and Mary Bubnik. "You're in charge of facials," Zan instructed Mary, "because you have a peaches-and-cream complexion."

"I do?" Mary replied, putting her hand to her cheek. "Why, thank you."

"What do you want me to do?" Rocky asked, slipping on the white smock and rolling up the sleeves.

"With your karate experience," Zan declared, "I'll bet you have really strong hands. So you're the *masseuse*."

"What's that?" Rocky narrowed her eyes. "It sounds like moose."

Zan laughed. "It's French for someone who does massage therapy. That'll be your department."

"But I don't know how to do massages."

"There's nothing to it," Zan said. "It's like kneading dough and doing karate chops."

Rocky sliced at the air with her hands. "I guess I can handle that."

Gwen and McGee stepped through the open front door and Gwen demanded, "What do you mean, Fit 'n' Trim Health Spa?"

"Follow me." Zan smiled mysteriously as she led them toward the kitchen.

Gwen noticed the white coats the girls were wearing and grumbled, "I don't like the looks of this."

The sight of the kitchen didn't make her feel any better. The breakfast table had been cleared off and a stack of fluffy white towels lay next to a huge array of cold creams, moisturizers, and liniments. A large rolling pin, a big roll of plastic wrap, and another of tin foil sat beside two pairs of yellow rubber gloves. Several large pots full of suspicious-looking concoctions burbled softly on the stove.

"Welcome," Zan said with a sweeping gesture, "to my beautification chamber."

"It looks more like a torture chamber," Gwen grumbled.

"This is great!" McGee exclaimed.

"I had so much fun doing my research," Zan said, pointing to the fashion and health magazines strewn across the white counter top. "The hardest part was deciding which weight-loss program to use."

Over in the corner an exercise bike and a rowing machine stood waiting. A poster with workout instructions was taped across the venetian blinds on the window.

Gwen could feel her stomach start to churn. It always did that when she got nervous.

"I must have read fifty magazines," Zan continued, "but I finally found the miracle treatment. You're guaranteed to lose ten pounds in ten minutes."

"Ten minutes?" Gwen gasped, backing toward the door. "What is it?"

Zan grinned and held up three rolls of Ace bandages and a pair of scissors. "The mummy wrap!"

Chapter Eleven

"I can't breathe!" Gwen gasped as billowing clouds of steam filled the bathroom. After Zan had turned on the hot water taps in the sink and bathtub, Rocky and McGee shoved Gwen into the tiny room and locked the door.

"You're not supposed to breathe," Zan explained from outside in the hall. "The steam makes the pores of your skin open up." Holding the latest issue of *Glamour Girl* magazine in her hands, Zan read loudly, "The toxins must be removed before the mummy wrap can be applied."

"Look!" Gwen pointed to her arms. "They're removed. They're running down my arm."

McGee, who'd remained in the bathroom with Gwen, said, "That's just sweat."

"Perfect," Zan cried. "That means all the dirt is coming out."

"This whole thing is totally gross," Gwen said. "I hate to sweat, I'm being blinded by steam, and I have decided I definitely don't need a mummy wrap."

The bathroom door flew open and banged against the wall. "You have to do the mummy wrap," Rocky declared. "Mary Bubnik and I have been mixing up the ingredients." She carried a tray into the room and set it on the bathroom sink.

"Wait!" Zan cried. "We can't do the wrap yet. The bandages have to soak in the mixture for ten minutes."

"Good," McGee said, "that will be just enough time for a Jacuzzi."

"What's that?" Mary Bubnik asked.

"It's a whirlpool soak for athletes with tired muscles."

"Well, my muscles are exhausted," Gwen said, dashing for the door and inhaling the cool air outside the bathroom, "but I am definitely not an athlete."

"Don't worry," McGee said, "we'll make you one yet." She pulled Gwen over to the bathtub.

"Did I say I was worried?" Gwen protested. "I could go the rest of my life and not be an athlete. It wouldn't bother me a bit."

McGee wasn't paying attention. "We need something to make the water churn," she said to Zan.

"How about an electric fan?" Mary Bubnik suggested.

"Are you out of your mind?" Gwen shrieked. "You could electrocute someone that way."

"There might be something in the kitchen," Zan said thoughtfully. "I'll go see."

McGee dragged the stool over to the bathtub and said, "Sit here while the water fills up."

"I'm not getting into that bathtub." Gwen crossed her arms stubbornly. "And that's final."

"OK, you don't have to put your whole body into it," McGee said, "but you can at least put your legs in."

"Yeah," Rocky agreed. "Since you want to strengthen your ankles and slim down your calves, that would be fine."

Gwen hesitated. She knew that she wouldn't be able to escape getting wet, so soaking her legs sounded a lot better than her whole body. "OK, but only for a short while, and if I start sweating again, then I stop."

McGee leaned over and flipped the faucet on full. As she did her arm caught the towels piled next to the bathtub and they fell into the water.

"These are soaked," Rocky said, pulling the heavy white towels out of the bathtub. "Zan!" she shouted out the door. "The towels got wet. What should I do with them?"

"Just put them in the hall," Zan shouted back from the kitchen.

Rocky took the four sopping bathtowels and piled them in a heap on the oriental carpet in the front hall.

"We found the perfect thing," Mary Bubnik said, skipping into the room. "An old egg-beater."

Zan held it up for all to see. "It's hand-operated. You just turn the handle and the water churns."

"Okay, Gwen, put your legs in the water," McGee ordered. "I'll run the Jacuzzi." She grabbed the egg beater from Zan and, sticking it in the water, spun the handle furiously. Gwen pulled her sweatpants up over her knees and then gingerly stepped into the bathtub. The frothy water swirled in and around her calves.

"While your legs are getting in shape," Rocky said to Gwen, "we'll apply your mummy wrap and facial." She was dipping long lengths of Ace bandage in the mixing bowl on the tray as she talked.

Gwen eyed the big bowl warily. "What's on those bandages?"

"Truly wonderful ingredients," Zan replied. "All part of a secret recipe."

"That's right," Mary Bubnik agreed. "Oatmeal, spinach, herbal tea, and molasses."

"That makes me want to barf!" Gwen said.

"Don't worry," Rocky said as she pulled another long bandage out of the bowl and handed it to Zan. "You don't eat it, you wear it."

"Hold your arms down by your sides." Zan wrapped the saturated strip around Gwen's body, starting with her neck. "And keep very still. This will compress everything and make you pounds thinner."

"Like magic," Mary Bubnik giggled.

"I don't feel very magical," Gwen grumbled, as they wound the bandages around and around her body, pinning her arms to her sides. They finally tied it off just below her knees. "I feel like I'm trapped inside a giant oatmeal and spinach cookie."

"You look thinner already," McGee said, taking a rest from working the Jacuzzi. She patted Gwen on the shoulder and a sticky mess of oatmeal and molasses clung to her hand. "Gooey, but thinner."

Zan was very pleased with how well her health spa was going. She clapped her hands and announced, "And now for the mud pack."

"Mixed especially for you by me," Mary Bubnik said proudly.

"Is it really mud?" Gwen asked.

"Of course." Mary carried the bowl over to Gwen's side. "I found it in the back alley of the apartment building." She scooped her hands into the mixture and slopped a big handful onto Gwen's cheek.

"That's ice cold!" Gwen squealed.

"It's good for your face," Zan said with authority. "It closes the pores."

"Mine just slammed shut," Gwen grumbled. "And now my face itches, and my hands are tied." She squirmed and wriggled her arms. "Oooh, someone itch my nose, please."

As Zan delicately scratched the tip of Gwen's nose, Gwen's glasses slid forward precariously. Zan took them off and Gwen groaned, "Oh, great, now I'm blind! This *is* a torture chamber."

"Re-laaaax," Mary said soothingly. She rubbed her palm in a circular motion across Gwen's cheeks and forehead. "This is also a facial massage."

"Is mud good for the hair?" McGee asked. " 'Cause you're getting it all over Gwen's."

"Yuck!" Gwen said.

"Don't move your mouth," Rocky commanded. "That stuff has to dry on there."

"Maybe we should put a towel on her head," Zan suggested.

"Those got all wet," McGee said. "Have you got anything else we could use?"

"My mom has an old scarf hanging on a hook in the hall," Zan replied. "We can use that to tie her hair back."

Moments later, Zan returned with a long filmy scarf covered with geometric designs. Rocky looked at it and asked, "You sure your mom won't mind us using it?"

Zan shook her head. "She never wears it. It's been hanging there for years." She tied the scarf around Gwen's head and carefully tucked her hair inside it.

"This reminds me of when we used to make mud pies in Oklahoma," Mary Bubnik giggled as she smeared another glop of mud on Gwen's face. As she scooped up another handful of mud, she looked down at her palm and her laughter stopped.

"Oh, ick!"

She threw the bowl in the air and it crashed onto the floor, splattering mud everywhere. Mary Bubnik didn't stop to pick it up but ran in a little circle, yelling, "Ick! Ick! Ick!"

"Mary, look what you did!" McGee shouted. "What's the matter with you?"

"A worm!" was all Mary could gasp before she ran across the floor out of the bathroom. Then she pounded down the hall to the kitchen, leaving a trail of footprints on the carpet.

Gwen, who had been concentrating on keeping her face still, screeched, "A worm? Get it off of me!" She leaned over to dunk her head in the bath water and the painted scarf sank to the bottom of the tub.

"Don't move!" McGee shouted. "I see the worm. It's on the floor, right here." She picked up the squirming creature by one end and held it in front of Rocky's face.

"Get it away from me!" Rocky shouted. "I hate those things!" She dropped the tray full of mummy wrap ingredients with a crash and ran for the kitchen. The jars and bowls rolled across the floor out into the hallway.

"Geez Louise, Rocky," McGee said hurrying after her with the worm still in her hand. "I never thought *you*'d be afraid of a little old worm."

"I'm not," Rocky replied, peering around the kitchen door. "I just don't like them thrust in my face. And don't come any closer!"

"Oh, no!" Zan dropped to her knees on the hall carpet where the spilled jars had made an ugly stain. "I've got to wipe this up before my mother gets home." She stood up and ran for the kitchen.

By now Rocky, McGee, and Mary Bubnik had all tracked mud into the kitchen and the tile floor was as slick as ice.

"I need paper towels and cleanser quick— *yiiieeeee!*" Zan's feet flew out from under her, and she slid across the floor toward the open pantry door. She hit it with all her weight and the door snapped off its hinges.

Meanwhile Gwen had managed to get out of the tub and she hopped into the hallway. "Get me out of this mummy wrap," she cried. "I can't move." She stumbled and fell against the white wall. "Now I can't stand up." Gwen flipped her body helplessly along the wall, leaving a zig-zag trail of green sticky smears as she tried to push herself back to an upright position.

"*What* in the *world* is going on here?"

At the sound of Mrs. Reed's outraged voice in the hall, Zan and the girls froze in their tracks.

"What are these soggy towels doing on my oriental rug?"

None of them dared reply. Mrs. Reed stomped out of the foyer into the hall and ran right into Gwen, who was leaning helplessly against the wall. "Gwendolyn? My God, what happened to you?"

Gwen opened her mouth to explain but was cut off by another anguished cry from Mrs. Reed. "Mud... footprints.... What's happened to my walls? And my white carpet? This house is a disaster!"

She rushed past Gwen to the bathroom. Mary Bubnik, who had ducked behind the butcher block in the kitchen, whispered to McGee, "Do you think she'll notice that we left the bathwater running?"

Another shriek split the air.

"I think she noticed," McGee whispered back.

"The bathroom is flooded!" Mrs. Reed groaned. "And my beautiful hand-painted scarf... ruined!"

Rocky tugged at Zan's sleeve. "Is there a back exit out of here? I think maybe we should just leave quietly."

"Suzannah D. Reed! I want an explanation, and I want it *now!*"

106

"Too late," McGee moaned.

"What does the D stand for?" Mary Bubnik asked.

Zan stood up and swallowed hard. "Dead duck."

She led her three friends into the living room. Mrs. Reed stood with her arms crossed and her lips tightly pursed. A tiny muscle on her face twitched as she clenched and unclenched her jaw.

Zan stared at her mother in a panic. She knew Mrs. Reed would explode in a moment and embarrass her in front of her friends. Part of Zan wished her friends would just disappear but the other part of her wanted them to stay, because she dreaded what would happen after they left.

Mrs. Reed took a step toward the girls, and they all flinched. Then the doorbell rang. Zan's mother stared at them coldly for a moment, then disappeared into the foyer. Rocky heaved a sigh of relief. "Saved by the bell."

McGee checked her watch and groaned. "Not likely. That's Gwen's mother coming to pick us up. Geez Louise, are we going to get it!"

Mrs. Reed ushered Mrs. Hays into the living room and pointed at the four girls in white jackets covered in mud and oatmeal.

"Oh, Mary, this is awful," Gwen's mother gasped. "I promise you, Gwendolyn will be punished severely for her part in this catastrophe." Then she spun in a circle, a confused look on her face. "Where *is* Gwendolyn?"

"Somebody help me!"

There was a loud clunk as Gwen finally lost her footing and fell to the floor. Then she rolled herself across the soggy carpet out into the living room. Mrs. Hays took one look at her and declared, "You are not getting in my nice new car looking like that, young lady. You march yourself into the bathroom right now, before you ruin the rest of Mrs. Reed's carpet."

"March?" Gwen lifted her head off the floor and squinted at her mother. "I can't even walk. And if someone doesn't get me out of this mummy wrap this instant, I'm going to scream!"

The girls ran forward and took Gwen back into the bathroom where they removed her bandages. Gwen was so furious that she refused to even look at them. She just sat on the stool and stared straight ahead. To everyone's dismay, the spinach and molasses had soaked through the bandages and completely stained her clothes.

"P.U." Mary pinched her nose shut and murmured, "That stuff's really starting to smell." Zan grabbed a can of air freshener from the closet and sprayed the room but that only added a sweet floral scent to the awful stench.

Mrs. Hays appeared at the bathroom door. "Girls, Mrs. Reed is calling your mothers to explain why you will be late getting home this evening."

"Late?" McGee asked.

"Of course," Mrs. Hays replied. "You're not going anywhere until this mess is cleaned up and the house is absolutely spotless."

"But what am I supposed to do?" Gwen's chin began to tremble. "I feel awful, and I don't have any clothes to wear."

Mrs. Hays smiled thinly. "I think Mary Reed and I can come up with a solution to that problem."

An hour and a half later a strange procession headed out the front entrance of the Reed's apartment building.

"I have never been so humiliated in my entire life," Gwen muttered as Rocky and McGee helped her hop down the steps. Her mother had made her step into a large green garbage bag and tied it around her shoulders.

She stared miserably out at the neighbor kids, who'd gathered to watch her hop to the car. As Mrs. Hays maneuvered her daughter into the back seat, she hissed, "Don't even think about moving a muscle until we get home."

The rear window had been rolled down to air out the awful smell of spinach and molasses. Gwen sat alone in stony silence, trying to ignore the sticky feeling of her clothes inside the garbage bag. The others had decided to ask Mrs. Bubnik for a ride. As the Cadillac pulled away, Gwen glared at her friends on the sidewalk and announced, "I will never, *ever* forgive any of you for this as long as I live."

Chapter Twelve

On Saturday, Rocky stomped into the dressing room at the ballet studio and slammed the little wooden box on the table. "This stone is cursed. You can have it."

Mary Bubnik, who had been the first to arrive, was sitting on the bench putting on her ballet slippers. She looked up, flabbergasted. "How can you say that about the Sacred Stone of Anastasia?"

"Because of this." Rocky took off her sunglasses and shoved her face up close to Mary Bubnik's. Her right eye was swollen with a huge purple and green bruise.

"Oh, Rocky, that's just terrible," Mary Bubnik cried. "Does it hurt?"

Rocky shrugged. "It did at first, but not anymore."

"I can't believe that boy Russell punched you in the eye. He must be terrible."

"He is." Rocky slumped down on one of the benches. "I took that stone to school with me —"

"To apologize?"

"Are you kidding? I thought I didn't need to since I had the lucky stone." Rocky untied her red high-tops and slipped them into her dance bag. "So I asked the assistant principal if I could make an important announcement over the loud speaker."

"They let students do that at your school?"

"Sure. It's called the living newspaper. At the start of each day kids make announcements about bake sales and games, sing Happy Birthday to friends. Things like that."

"What did you say?"

"I said I wanted the whole school to know that Russell Stokes was a complete slime and a total liar. I was going to say more, but the assistant principal took the microphone away from me."

"I can't believe you did that!" Mary's hands flew to her face. "I never would have had the courage."

Rocky pulled her wild black hair into a ponytail on the side. "It was nothing."

Mary Bubnik stared at Rocky for a long moment. Finally she said, "I hate to say this, but I think I understand why Russell punched you."

"I'm not sure it was Russell," Rocky said. "It was

111

a whole bunch of guys who jumped me. It could have been some of his buddies." She shoved the box angrily across the dressing table. "But that stupid stone didn't protect me one bit."

Just then the curtain flew open and Gwen charged into the dressing room. Zan and McGee were right behind her. "I can't believe it!" Gwen shouted, tossing her blue canvas dance bag onto one of the benches. "I just can't believe it."

"What?" Rocky and Mary asked.

"After all the torture and humiliation you guys put me through with the Fit 'n' Trim Mummy Museum ... and then having to ride home sweating in an awful garbage bag." Gwen shuddered at the memory. "After all that — I *gained* two pounds!"

"Well, if it makes you feel any better," Zan murmured as she slumped against one of the lockers, "my mother grounded me for a month. I can't go anywhere except to school and ballet lessons."

"A whole month?" Rocky gasped. "Boy, she's as strict as my dad."

Sergeant Garcia was legendary for the stiff punishment he doled out. If Rocky or one of her four brothers stepped out of line, her father put them under "house arrest," or assigned them to KP — Kitchen Police — which meant they had to do the dishes for all seven Garcias for an entire week.

"It's that stupid stone," Rocky grumbled. "It's useless."

112

"Now that's not true," Mary Bubnik protested. "It worked great for Zan and me."

"I'm starting to have some doubts about the powers of the stone," Zan admitted. "Maybe it truly is an ordinary chipped rock, and Miss Delacorte made up the story about it just to give me confidence. The words I spelled weren't terribly hard."

"Don't say that!" Mary Bubnik protested. "Look what it did for McGee."

McGee sat slumped on the bench, staring at her tennis shoes. "The stone didn't do a thing for me."

"What do you mean?" Mary Bubnik looked thoroughly confused. "I thought you made the baseball team."

"I made the team." McGee kicked at the floor with the edge of her sneaker. "But not the Bombers. They stuck me on the worst team in the league. Now we're going to get creamed."

"I wish y'all wouldn't talk like that," Mary said, her face growing redder and redder. "You're going to bring a curse on us."

"We're already cursed." Rocky grabbed the wooden box and opened the lid. "This stone has brought us nothing but bad luck." To Mary's horror Rocky lifted the stone off its velvet cushion and flung it across the room. It bounced off the wall and ricocheted out of sight behind the standing mirror.

"Rocky, how could you!" Mary gasped. "What about our toe shoes?"

At that moment the curtain swept open and Page Tuttle and Alice Wescott sauntered into the dressing room. The gang shut up immediately and finished changing their clothes in silence.

Mary Bubnik fought hard to keep the tears from her eyes. She believed in the Sacred Stone of Anastasia with all of her heart, and now it was lying in the dust somewhere in the dressing room. There was no way she could look for it in front of the Bunheads. Mary Bubnik decided to wait until everyone had left the dressing room before retrieving it.

But when it was time for ballet class to begin, Rocky stood at the curtain and called, "Mary, are you coming?"

Mary Bubnik took one last look around the room and then hurried out of the dressing room. "If I can't find it," she told herself, "maybe no one else will."

When they entered the studio Annie Springer was already there, conferring with Mr. Anton.

"What's *he* doing here?" McGee muttered.

"He hasn't finished the exam," Zan whispered back. "Remember? He said he wanted to re-test a few people."

The scale sat on the floor between Annie and Mr. Anton, glistening in the light. Just looking at it made Gwen's blood run cold. The director had been unhappy with her weight last week. *Wait till he sees how much you've gained* this *week,* a little voice inside of her warned.

114

Without a moment's hesitation Gwen turned and ran back to the dressing room. She hurried behind the standing mirror where she'd left her clothes and threw her pink overalls and sweatshirt on over her leotard and tights.

"I'm getting out of this place," Gwen announced to the empty room. "And I'm never coming back!"

Gwen grabbed her dance bag and raced for the front door of the academy. She had one foot over the doorsill when a voice called, "Gwendolyn! Where are you go-ink?"

"Out," Gwen replied as she spun around and faced Miss Delacorte. "For a pizza and an order of fries."

Miss Delacorte put one hand to her chest in dismay. "How will you be able to dance with all of that in your tummy?"

"I won't," Gwen mumbled, "and that suits me just fine."

"My goodness!" Miss Delacorte made little clucking sounds as she shook her head. "You sound so unhappy. Can you tell me what is the matter?"

"Your stupid Stone of Anastasia!" Gwen burst out. "That's what's the matter."

"What do you mean?"

"I tried believing in it to get my toe shoes, and all I got was humiliation."

"Oh, my, there has been a terrible misunderstanding." Miss Delacorte took Gwen by the shoulders and led her to the couch.

"No kidding," Gwen said bitterly. "You said the stone was magical, and it isn't. It's just a big fake."

"No, no, that is not true." Miss Delacorte flipped the end of her lavender scarf over her shoulder and whispered, "The stone has great powers—"

"Ha!" Gwen folded her arms across her chest and stuck out her lower lip.

"Please, you must listen." Miss Delacorte took Gwen's hand in hers. "But the stone's magic will only help those who help themselves."

"You're just making excuses for it," Gwen said, pulling her hand away.

"Maybe I am." Miss Delacorte stood up abruptly and when she spoke again, her voice was full of hurt. "But I must say this. Before you judge the stone and its powers, ask yourself a few questions. Have you done your best? And if you haven't — are you putting the blame on someone else? Look to your heart, Gwendolyn."

"Right now I'm going to look to my stomach," Gwen retorted. "I'll see you later."

With that she ran out of the academy and down the corridor to the stairway. Gwen hurtled out the front entrance, straight down the one hundred and two steps in front of Hillberry Hall, and didn't stop till she reached the corner. She ducked into the alley and leaned against the wall to catch her breath.

"Gwen?" a tiny voice called. "Is that you?"

Gwen spun around so fast she nearly fell over. There was no one in the alley. "Oh, great!" she moaned. "Now I'm hearing voices."

"I'm up here on the fire escape."

Gwen shielded her eyes from the sun and squinted up at the side of the building. Julie McKenna sat hugging her knees to her chest on the platform of an old rusty fire escape.

"Julie?" Gwen put her hands on her hips. "What are you doing up there?"

"Hiding." Julie flashed a shy smile. "You see, I started to go into class but when I saw Mr. Anton, I" — she shrugged her thin shoulders — "I just wasn't ready to face him again so soon."

Gwen nodded. "Same here."

Julie climbed down the ladder and hopped to the ground. "I've been working out all week with weights but it's hard to make real progress in such a short time."

"Weights?" Gwen tilted her head. "You mean, like at a gym?"

"In the physical therapy room at the hospital," Julie replied. "My doctor arranged to let me use it."

"Doctor? Are you sick?"

"I was. My parents used to be reporters. They worked all over the world when I was very little, and I got polio."

"Wow!" Gwen shook her head. "I didn't know people still got that."

"My parents thought that, too. It was a big shock to them." She said sheepishly. "And me."

"Gosh, you don't look like you have any problems," Gwen blurted out. "I — I mean, you're not in a wheelchair, or wearing leg braces, or anything awful like that."

"No, not any more." Julie smiled. "But I used to. I've spent most of my life in and out of hospitals. At one point the doctors were sure I'd never walk again. But see?" Julie leaped lightly over the mud puddle running down the middle of the alley. "I fooled them."

Gwen watched the frail dark-haired girl dancing in the alley and tried to imagine how hard her life must have been when she was struggling to walk. Suddenly worrying about her own weight seemed kind of foolish. That was definitely a problem Gwen could solve herself, and she didn't have to go to hospital therapy rooms to do it.

"I've never had anything like that happen to me," Gwen said. "I sprained my wrist once, but that doesn't really count for much."

Julie kicked her legs high in the air. "I still get tired easily, but I just know I could get my feet strong enough for toe shoes, if Mr. Anton would give me a little more time."

"I don't know if extra time would do me any good,"

118

Gwen muttered. "I'm fat. And that's all there is to it."

"That's not true." Julie, who had been in a lunge position stretching her calves, straightened up. "I'll bet that, if you cut out snacks and just worked out a little, you could get into shape pretty easily."

"What kind of workout?" Gwen asked warily, remembering the horrible things she had gone through with McGee on the obstacle course and then at Zan's house.

"Oh, maybe just a few more dance classes a week, and some extra sit-ups."

"Gee, that doesn't sound too bad."

"That's what I'm going to do," Julie said excitedly. "Maybe we could take the classes together."

Gwen wasn't about to commit herself to spending more time at the ballet studio when she had just sworn never to return there again. "Um, I'll have to think about it, OK?"

"Sure." Julie leaped back over the mud puddle. "In the meantime, do you want to have a soda or something." She gestured toward Hillberry Hall. "I mean, we can't really go back in there. And it's almost an hour till my mom picks me up."

For the first time that day, Gwen smiled. "I know the perfect place. Follow me."

Gwen skipped down the alley, pausing just long enough to empty a couple of items into an open dumpster. One of them was a pack of Twinkies; the other was a half-empty bag of M&Ms.

The two girls raced across the street to the little restaurant with the red-and-white sign. Gwen shoved open the door and the brass bell announced their arrival.

"Hi, Hi!" Gwen shouted gleefully. "I have someone I really want you to meet."

Hi Lo was sitting at the counter with his little wire-rim glasses perched on his nose, reading the newspaper. He stood up and bowed formally. "I am always honored to meet a friend of Gwen's." Then he grinned and added, "Welcome to Hi Lo's Pizza and Chinese Food To Go." As the girls sat down on their stools, he set fresh paper placemats in front of them. "What can I get you? A double chocolate fudge surprise?"

He wiggled his eyebrows and Julie giggled, "That sounds delicious."

Hi looked at Gwen and asked, "Should I make two?"

Gwen hesitated for only a second. Then she said firmly, "No, thanks, Hi. I'll just have a diet cola."

Chapter
Thirteen

The following Saturday Zan met Rocky, McGee, and Mary Bubnik at Hi Lo's for an emergency meeting. It had been almost a week since any of them had seen or heard from Gwen.

"I tried to call her," Mary Bubnik said as they huddled around the counter that morning, "but never got any answer. Do you think she's gone?"

McGee shook her head. "Gwen's not gone. She's just not answering the phone. I finally reached her mom, and Mrs. Hays said that Gwen didn't feel like talking to anyone."

"What do you think happened?" Rocky asked, taking a long sip of her Coke.

"I think she's truly upset about the toe shoes," Zan replied. "More than any of us realized."

"I don't blame her," McGee said. "If she doesn't get them, she'll have to be transferred to another class."

Mary Bubnik gasped in surprise. "I didn't know that."

"That's what Courtney and the Bunheads said." McGee jabbed at her ice with a straw. "And I'm afraid it's true."

Rocky set her glass down on the counter. "This is really serious. It could break up the gang."

"We can't let that happen," Mary Bubnik cried. "We just can't!"

"Well, Geez Louise, what are we supposed to do?" McGee said. "Refuse to get toe shoes?"

"We may have to," Zan said softly. "If we get them, and Gwen doesn't, that means she's out in the cold."

"This is terrible." Rocky slammed her fist on the table. "If we don't get toe shoes, the Bunheads will say we couldn't cut it."

"That's right," McGee groaned. "That'd be like admitting they were better than us."

"I wish there was some way we could help Gwen," Zan said.

"We tried to," McGee replied. "And look at the thanks we got. She won't even answer the phone."

"Well, do you blame her?" Mary Bubnik drawled.

"We put her through boot camp, wrapped her up in goo, and all she got out of it was two more pounds."

Suddenly Rocky leaped off her stool and faced the front door. "What was that?"

Before the others could answer, Rocky dropped to her knees and crawled to the big picture window. She raised her head slowly above the sill and peered through the glass. "I guess it was nothing."

"What are you so jumpy about?" McGee asked.

"Russell Stokes." Rocky opened the door and looked outside. "He's been following me, and I'm starting to think I see him wherever I go."

"Rocky, this is silly." Mary Bubnik put her hands on her hips. "Why don't you just give him back his dumb old schoolbooks, and then you won't have to worry anymore?"

"You really took his schoolbooks?" McGee asked, raising an eyebrow. "You mean he wasn't lying that day in the park?"

"I *accidentally* took his books," Rocky corrected. "Then one thing led to another, and now I don't know *what* to do."

"Give them back," Mary Bubnik said. "And apologize."

"No way!" Rocky snapped. "Everyone at school will think I'm a wimp."

Hi, who was wiping off the table in the back booth with a damp cloth, said, "You know, that reminds me of an old proverb I once read." He shut his eyes and recited, "To admit you are wrong when you are wrong is a sign of strength, not weakness. Your enemies will respect you for it."

"Where'd you read that?" Zan asked. "In some book by Confucius?"

Hi shook his head. "No, in a fortune cookie I got at Chan's China Dragon." The old man grinned. "Pretty good, isn't it?"

"Well, wherever you read it," Mary Bubnik said, "I think it's perfectly true. And I think Rocky should call Russell."

"You mean, talk to him on the phone?" Rocky turned visibly pale. "I — I can't."

"If you don't," Zan pointed out, "you'll just get more and more jumpy. I read about it in this psychology book. You just told us you're hearing and seeing things that aren't there. Well, that will just get worse, and before you know it, you'll have a nervous breakdown."

"Nervous breakdown!" Mary Bubnik gasped. "Oh, Rocky, call him right now."

Rocky shook her head stubbornly. "I can't."

"Why not?" McGee challenged.

"I don't know his number."

"Call information," Zan suggested.

Rocky still didn't budge.

McGee flipped up the visor of her baseball cap. "Maybe you *are* just a wimp," she said quietly.

Rocky's head flew up and her eyes flashed with

anger. "Nobody calls me a wimp and lives to tell about it."

McGee held up both hands. "Prove that you're not. I double-dare you to call him."

Rocky hesitated. She never passed up a dare, let alone a double-dare. Finally she set her jaw and marched behind the counter. Hi met her at the swinging door with the phone in his hand.

"Just dial information," he said with a smile, "and tell the operator his name." Before Rocky could say a word, Hi disappeared into the back room.

Rocky got Russell's number from the operator and wrote it on the little chalkboard above the counter. She took a deep breath and cracked her knuckles. "Here goes!"

The three other girls gathered around her, trying to listen.

"Come on, you guys," Rocky protested, "this isn't a party line." She pushed open the swinging door and carried the phone into the privacy of the kitchen.

"What if he's not there?" Mary Bubnik whispered.

"What if he *is* there?" McGee replied. "And threatens to break her kneecaps?"

"How can you say that?" Zan hissed. "You're the one who dared her to make the call."

"You're the one who said she was going to have a nervous breakdown," McGee shot back. "Besides, I think she should call. I'm just not positive it will all turn out that great."

They leaned their ears against the swinging door, hoping to catch a few words of the conversation. Rocky's voice could be heard from time to time but it was impossible to make out exactly what she was saying.

Then McGee heard the little ding of the receiver, indicating that the call was over. "She hung up."

Quick as a wink the girls dashed back around the counter and leaped onto their stools. When Rocky stepped back through the swinging door, she found three innocent faces staring at her.

"Well?" Mary Bubnik asked. "What did he say?"

Rocky shrugged impassively. "He said he's glad I admitted taking his books 'cause his teachers were getting pretty upset with him. But he wasn't too happy about the announcement I made in school."

"So is he going to break your kneecaps?" Mary Bubnik asked.

Rocky shook her head. "No. Russell thought it was pretty cool that I had the courage to make an announcement right in front of the principal. He even said he was sorry about my black eye." Her face lit up in a big smile. "And he wants me to meet him at Scooter's Video Arcade after school on Monday."

"Is that where he'll break your kneecaps?" Mary Bubnik asked.

"No!" Rocky laughed. "That's where he'll buy me a Coke and an order of nachos."

"A date!" all three girls shrieked at once. "You've got a date!"

Rocky slipped back onto the worn leather stool and grinned. "Yeah, it's kind of amazing, huh?"

Hi Lo stuck his head through the pick-up window. "Did you reach your enemy Mr. Russell Stokes?"

"Yes," Rocky said, her cheeks turning bright pink.

"And he's no longer her enemy," Mary Bubnik gushed, "he's her boyfriend."

The old man's face creased into a thousand merry wrinkles. "Boyfriend? This is very good news. Maybe I should fix us all a Super Dooper Hi Lo special to celebrate."

"We may have to postpone our celebrating," Zan declared solemnly. "We've got a more important problem to solve. Gwen."

McGee nodded. "If we get our toe shoes, we lose Gwen as a friend."

"And that would be just awful," Mary Bubnik cried.

"I mean, why did we take those classes in the first place?" Rocky asked. "To become a bunch of twinkle-toes?"

"No way." McGee shook her head.

"We took them because we liked each other," Zan answered, "and we wanted to stay together."

"Right!" McGee banged her fist on the counter. "Now look what's happening. We're letting Mr. Anton and the academy break up our friendship."

"Just so we can parade around on the tips of our toes," Mary Bubnik added. "It's really kind of silly, isn't it?"

For a moment no one said a word. Suddenly McGee pushed her glass away and hopped off her stool. "Well, I know what I'm going to do."

"What's that?" Hi asked.

"I'm going to talk to Mr. Anton."

One by one the girls met her determined look and stood up. With a farewell wave to Hi Lo they left the restaurant and marched across the street to the Deerfield Academy of Dance.

Chapter Fourteen

McGee led the four girls past Miss Delacorte at the reception desk straight into Mr. Anton's office. They had never stepped foot in there before, and it was very intimidating. The academy director was working on some papers at his desk, a pair of glasses perched on the end of his nose. Everything in the room was black or white, from the black leather couch with the zebra striped pillows to the black lacquered desk with its stark white lamps.

The director looked up in surprise. "I didn't hear you knock."

"We didn't," McGee spoke up. "But this is an urgent matter, and we have to talk to you right away."

Mr. Anton slipped his glasses onto the top of his

head and fixed his steely blue eyes on them. "You're from Miss Springer's class, aren't you?"

"We were," Rocky declared. "But not any more. We quit."

Mr. Anton raised an eyebrow. "All four of you?"

They looked at each other one last time, then nodded.

"You see, we all joined that class so we could be together," Mary Bubnik explained, "and we liked it a lot—"

"Except for the Bunheads," Rocky muttered under her breath, and Zan nudged her hard with her elbow. "Well, it's true."

"Anyway," Mary continued, "Gwen is our best friend."

"And if she can't have toe shoes . . ." Zan started.

"Then we don't want them either," Rocky finished.

"But—" Mr. Anton started to speak, but McGee cut him off.

"I know it means being demoted to a class with younger girls," she said in a rush. "And having the Bunheads make fun of us, but that doesn't matter."

"Because our friendship is more important than toe shoes," Zan declared.

"Or the Bunheads," Rocky added.

"So you can throw us out of the school, or put us in another class," Mary Bubnik said tearfully. "But please let us stay together!"

Mr. Anton stared at them in astonishment. Finally he clasped his hands together on his desk and asked, "Are you quite finished?"

The girls nodded timidly.

"Good. Because I believe none of this sacrifice is really necessary." A tiny smile flickered across his lips. "You see, Gwendolyn has been taking extra classes all this week."

"What?" the girls gasped in shock.

Mr. Anton nodded. "Miss Jo and the other teachers say they have already noticed a marked improvement. Gwen has even signed up for our Eat Light to Dance Right weight control program."

"Are we talking about the same person?" McGee asked in confusion. "Gwendolyn Hays? Short red hair? Glasses? Slightly on the chunky side?"

Mr. Anton leaned back in his chair. "Yes. I'm very impressed by her dedication. If all goes well, I see no reason why she shouldn't be able to go *en pointe* with the rest of you." He looked over their shoulders toward the door. "Isn't that right, Gwendolyn?"

The gang turned to see Gwen standing just inside the doorway. Her eyes glistened with tears. She tried several times to speak, but the words wouldn't come. Finally she was able to whisper, "Getting my toe shoes is wonderful, but having you guys for friends is the best thing of all."

Mary Bubnik was the first to hug her. Pretty soon

131

they were all in a clump with their arms wrapped around each other. They hopped in a circle, shouting, "Yea!"

On Monday afternoon, five happy girls stood in front of the mirror at Zimmerman's shoe store. Each was wearing a pair of shiny pink satin toe shoes. They locked hands and slowly raised up on their toes. For one brief moment they stood poised perfectly in the air. Then the smiles disappeared from their glowing faces.

"Ow!" McGee yelled. "These hurt!"

"I feel like I just stepped on an upside-down pin cushion," Mary Bubnik groaned.

Zan limped in a circle. "These must be ten sizes too small."

"That's how dancers wear them," an amused saleslady explained. "They should fit snugly."

"They're snug, all right," Rocky said, walking stiffly across the carpet. "My feet feel like they've been set in cement."

Gwen, who had struggled so hard for this moment, fought to keep a pleasant look on her face. "They're not so bad," she said in a pinched voice. "Once you get used to them." She lifted up on her toes and *bourréed* just like Courtney Clay around the side of the shoe rack. The moment she was out of sight Gwen dropped to her knees and groaned, "All of that agony — for *this?* I want a pizza."

From her position behind the shoe rack Gwen

could see Julie McKenna on the other side of the store. Mr. Anton had given her permission to have toe shoes, too. Julie twirled in little circles on the carpeted floor in front of the mirror.

"Show off," Gwen joked. Just then Julie spotted Gwen and waved. Gwen leaped to her feet and called out gaily, "Congratulations!"

"Thanks," Julie shouted back. "Aren't they wonderful?"

Gwen tried to agree, but the words that came out of her mouth were, "Yes, painful!"

By the time Gwen rejoined her friends they were all wrapping up their pink satin shoes in tissue and placing them back in their boxes. Gwen flopped into the nearest chair and with a sigh of relief removed her shoes.

Rocky replaced the lid of her shoe box and started to chuckle.

"What's so funny?" Gwen asked, rubbing her sore toes.

"I was just thinking about that stupid Stone of Anastasia," Rocky said. "It really didn't bring anybody luck."

"Oh, but it did!" Mary Bubnik declared. "It just took a little time."

"What do you mean?" Rocky demanded.

"Well, McGee's baseball team turned out to be great."

"That's true," McGee admitted. "We played our

first game on Thursday and stomped the Bombers, fifteen to three."

"And you're not fighting Russell Stokes anymore," Mary Bubnik added with a giggle. "You're dating him."

"Gee, I hadn't thought about that," Rocky said as they moved to the cash register.

Mary Bubnik set her shoe box on the counter. "And Gwen got her toe shoes."

"But Gwen was never the Keeper of the Stone," Zan pointed out. "So it couldn't have brought her luck."

"Besides," Gwen said as the saleslady rang up her purchase, "I've learned that, if you believe in yourself and work hard for what you want, you make your own good luck."

"That'll be twenty-one dollars and fifty cents," the saleslady announced.

Gwen reached into her coat pocket for the money her mother had given her. When she pulled out her hand, a shiny object flipped onto the counter. It landed on top of her toe shoes and lay glowing softly in the light.

"The Amber Stone of Anastasia!" Mary Bubnik breathed in awe.

Gwen spun to face her friends. "How did that get in my pocket?"

"I didn't put it there," Rocky protested.

"Me, neither," McGee said.

"It must have fallen on your coat," Zan whispered, "when Rocky threw it across the dressing room."

"But how could it have gotten inside my pocket?" Gwen asked as a chill ran up her spine.

Mary Bubnik's eyes were two big circles as she answered, "Magic."

The others weren't positive it was magic that had made Gwen the Keeper of the Stone, but just to be on the safe side. . . .

They quickly looked over their shoulders to make sure no one was watching. Then all four bowed in unison to the chipped little rock laying on top of the counter.

"Thank you, Amber Stone of Anastasia!" Zan murmured, "for bringing us our toe shoes."

"I'm sorry I ever doubted you," Gwen added quickly, "and I promise to return the M&Ms and Twinkies."

"And from now on," Mary Bubnik drawled, "we promise to protect you with our lives —"

Rocky and McGee joined in. "And believe in you with our hearts."

Bad News Ballet

Coming soon:
#6 Save D.A.D.!

"Well, look on the bright side," Rocky said, motion-ing for the gang to gather around her. "If there's no Deerfield Academy of Dance, there's no more dance classes."

"And no more lousy leotards," Gwen said em-phatically.

"But best of all," Rocky declared, "we wouldn't have to put up with the Bunheads!"

"Yea!" McGee cried, giving Rocky a high five.

Mary Bubnik, who had been very quiet for most of their conversation, said, "But aren't y'all forgetting something?"

"We wouldn't see each other anymore," Zan whis-pered, her deep brown eyes wide with alarm.

"Wow. I never thought about that." Gwen bit her lip worriedly.

"We have to figure out a way to save the acad-emy," Zan declared, her voice low and serious.